METATRON

THE CONFRONTATION

NOEL WILHELM MCDOUGALL

METATRON
THE CONFRONTATION

NOEL WILHELM McDOUGALL

Kravitz and Sons LLC
204 E Arlington Blvd. Suite B
Greenville, NC 27858

Published by Kravitz and Sons LLC.

ISBN: 979-8-89639-741-0 (sc)
ISBN: 979-8-89639-740-3 (e)

Library of Congress Control Number: 2026908698

Table of Contents

PROLOGUE:

We as human beings typically only understand what is perceived by the eyes rather than by the rational spirit. Keenness of understanding is due to keenness of vision. Sometimes our eyes see what the mind wants us to see but does not necessarily mean it is real.

When we see with the spirit, the greatest mysteries of creation are revealed and in return, that transform into wisdom.

This world of dust and bones is but an illusion but we did not come from this nature because we were created in the image of the lord and his kingdom perishes not; therefore, we are much more than our present existence.

There is a great difference between something impossible and something which has simply not yet happened. Mankind in its own nature avoids what it cannot understand since it has no control over the outcome, followed by chronic fear and paranoia, potentially driving one insane; however, the untold occurrence of what happened four years before the "war on terror", on two separate continents that spanned over a period of nine months is told in this story. Some of the occurrences happened eons ago and some have been kept hidden in government files up until the present day; nonetheless, let us meet, "the prince of presence"!

As the sun rose on the east behind the Indian ocean on a crisp Sunday morning, flight 360 a 767-airbus carrying government agent and anthropologist Clyde Harper and his two kids Lark and Chess who were scheduled to land at Heathrow international airport in the UK in 6 hours were being diverted.

A few minutes later, the pilots were notified that they were to turn northeast toward Thailand and await further instructions, a sudden burst of laser flashes hit the jet liner with high powered heat beams. Pilots were temporarily blinded but quickly regained their sight.

The plane shook quite intensely but quickly leveled out as control was regained but had caused paranoia for a few minutes onboard the aircraft.

Reports were coming to the pilots from ground level of multiple rockets being fired randomly from the middle east, but nothing was said about laser lights. Clyde Harper being connected to his wife Sky always, who happens to work for the FBI, repeatedly attempted to call her, but phone signals were not available. He wanted to make sure they were not in a dangerous situation. Clyde and his children, Chess and Lark, were originally from California but were constantly travelling due to work demand. The jetliner made it through the ordeal without suffering major problems, but the FAA was already investigating what had hit the plane. Pilots onboard were struck in awe as they could not understand where this phenomenon originated from, but it is believed by some government entities that a highly sophisticated weapon in development was being tested on human beings without regards for life by these heartless individuals because certain sections of the plane had burnt marks beneath, near the cargo area.

Clyde Harper and his youngsters made it to Heathrow international, United Kingdom for work issues then returned to California 8 days later where they reunited with his wife Sky with a barbeque scheduled for the upcoming Sunday with other relatives and acquaintances.

That very same Sunday May twenty third, 1998, Loretta Alcala, a citizen of Guatemala who was residing in Kito Ecuador attending a catholic training in mysticism and investigating a horrific local legend, so much so that even the president of that country was concerned but the country as one could not even begin to analyze this terrible menace.

Local legend says that a man of Mayan descent who lived in a small town in Guatemala with his then deceased wife and child dealt with witchcraft in attempt to bring her back from the dead after losing her to dengue fever but instead he was taken deep into the jungles by a malevolent entity due to failure in living up to a blood contract.

This incident occurred 150 years ago in the 19th century but whatever this dark spirit did to this man involved in witchery caused shockwaves throughout Guatemala and even neighboring countries as several nights out of the week exactly at what they called the heavy hour which is midnight in those places, entire families were taken from their homes and brutally skinned alive in the hills just outside the town limits. It was believed that the skin was used as gifts to please the prince of darkness as well as hatred toward humanity. The mystery was, who was responsible for such heinous crimes?

Was it the witch transformed into a powerful beast or was it the demon himself who had already murdered the individual involved in witchcraft and taken his soul?

Large numbers of brutal crimes were skyrocketing, dwindling the town's population until one morning the military acted.

Hundreds of Armed soldiers ordered by the government invaded the jungle in a hunt for this terrible menace but not a single soldier was ever heard from again. It was as if the jungle swallowed them, leaving nothing behind.

Meanwhile in eastern Europe a platoon of American soldiers along with French forces were investigating a rare occurrence in an Afghan village in which the entire population simply vanished into thin air overnight without even a trace. About eight hundred inhabitants had ceased to exist. Homes were empty but belongings were left behind as if they all ran away into the desert during the night in great haste.

The United States government was informed on the situation and experts on both crime and the supernatural were called into action.

The night American military had arrived on the scene of that town; satellite radar observations showed a strange vapor that seemed to originate from beneath the ground engulfing the entire village that reached about one thousand feet into the air. This phenomenon resembled the heat coming from the hood of a car on a sweltering day after being driven for a long distance.

Truly this was beyond the experts as they could not even begin to understand what took place; however, a medium present who had the ability to see things of the past without having to be there suspected that it was not caused by humans but by something not of this world. His counterpart in forensics raised the suspicion that terrorists were being supported by a brilliant Russian physicist scientist by the name of Matvey Lukenchoff who was believed to have acquired the ability to manipulate dark energy which is an invisible and undetected pervasive energy which fills the universe with as much as 68%. This energy has an antigravity effect which pushes planets apart; therefore, it is an extremely powerful force if not the most powerful in existence. Clyde Harper and his wife Sky were finally called in to assist with the eerie situation in this Afghan village. The very next day they both arrived on the scene and began the great task of unraveling the mystery. Sky was more of a secret agent responsible for keeping top information hidden from almost everyone. Clyde on the other hand decided to examine the ground beneath and what he found was shocking.

It appeared that 12 feet beneath that village was a huge tunnel stretching for hundreds of miles based on their calculations and examinations but the rover they sent down came to a sudden stop. Its mounted cameras captured what appeared to be black smoke or a dark fog which brought the rover to a stop about 28 miles underground inside this tunnel. They called in engineers from the army corps of engineers who sent down a robotic android which was developed by the US government under stealth operation. This cyborg was equipped with state-of-the-art technology capable of resisting heat and nuclear blast as well as armed with a 50-caliber machine gun mounted on its robotic arm.

As it descended into the tunnel, a loud thundering sound came from all sides surrounding the area shaking the ground above around all those present undertaking this task. Some were nervous and turned pale but most of them tried to ignore the sickening sound.

When the cyborg got to the area where the rover had stalled, it raised its flame thrower and fired it at the strange dark glow but just as it did, its camera captured a hideous creature like no other which appeared to walk right through the flames, extended its what seemed like claws in place of hands and latched on to the cyborg attempting to drag it away but it failed as it defended itself; unfortunately ,several other of these creatures arrived and dismantled the robotic hardware into pieces and ended up vanishing in a ball of fire along with the remnants of this weapon created by the United States. The camera was quite unstable but captured most of what occurred. all of this occurred in the earth's lithosphere, near the crust.

Just as Clyde Harper was going to draw to his conclusion, a huge ballistic missile landed about half a mile from them since they were in enemy territory with a giant explosion, sending shockwaves throughout a circumference area from the target but this was something to expect since it was a time of war. The assisting individuals supporting Clyde and his wife Sky, and the rest of the American team sent a distress signal for support in attempt to receive cover should another missile land on them. Clyde spoke to his wife Sky in a highly concerned tone of voice saying "honey; this is a fight we might not win"! these things beneath the ground are not a regular enemy. They think and they calculate. Sky lowered her gaze with an afflicted look; nevertheless, they decided to contact the white house and reveal the dire situation, they were facing. The US president reached out to its allies and the brightest minds in most parts of the globe, which was recommended by Clyde and his team, but when they were informed on the nature of the situation, Most refused to become involved except for one family known as, the Volcotrans. These folks were in essence, passivists and eerie, yet rare in appearance, almost intimidating and not involved whatsoever in the conflicts of the world.

They were immigrants from Romania who lived deep in the redwood forest in Orick California near the Oregon border. Adrien and Adelina along with their son Cole who strangely had a very pale complexion almost like a ghost and was constantly travelling back and forth between the US and Romania. It was later understood that he was not a true relative to the Volkotrans but rather a youth of around nineteen years of age who was picked up off the streets of Budapest by this strange couple.

The Volcotrans answered the call of the president and agreed to speak on what they knew but requested eight days for them to prepare for what they had to say and revealed to the white house that what they had to say must be revealed globally because what is coming; the world may not survive.

Clyde and his team were told to return to the US a couple days later. They arrived in Washington DC on a Saturday and His presence was requested at the white house the very same day. Sky on the other hand was requested to meet with a NASA official in relation to the destroyed robot inside the tunnels beneath the Afghan town.

Clyde urged government officials to speak on the nature of the volcotrans about who they were and why they were so interested in assisting without being involved in any government agency.

He said to them; "if you guys know something important about who these people are, it is your duty to inform the experts and the military about what might be going on! Why did they say that we all might not survive what is coming?"

Allan Mateman' a nerdy newcomer to work for the government was:

well, his name said it all; he was constantly Horney being an unmarried single man of thirty-six years replied, "I'll tell you what is coming! It is the end of the world, that is what! It won't be long before we see dead people crawling out of their tombs and start to eat us alive, and what is worse is that I haven't even slept with a woman, and I might die this way"!

"Mateman: shut it, or you will be the first to be eaten"!

Replied another official.

The president and his team decided to allow the Volcotrans to say what they needed in a request directly from the white house. They were instructed to be in Washington DC the very next day but the Volcotrans stated that they needed 3 days because they needed to communicate with an acquaintance in central America directly connected with what they intended to do.

Loreta Alcala was in the middle of a conversation with a renowned priest in Kito Ecuador discussing on what can be done regarding the devil living deep in the jungle devouring people almost daily.

By this time since the incidents in Afghanistan and the situation with the Volcotrans in the US, 3 weeks had passed. The entire country of Guatemala was in panic mode requesting assistance from neighboring territories but many of their cries for assistance went unanswered since these other territories had problems of their own; hence, the effects of the war on terror was on the minds of many across the globe. When Loretta answered, she immediately spoke in a completely unknown language. Clearly it was the Volcotrans on the other end of the line, but why would they call Mrs. Alcala and what connections did they have together? Loretta apologized to the priest for the interruption and told him she had to leave for the US immediately but assured they will find a way to put an end to the evil living deep in the jungle upon her return.

She boarded a commercial jetliner during the overnight hours from Kito to Sacramento California, obviously heading to the residence of the Volcotrans in Orick California in the redwood forest. Upon arrival at the residence, she did something very strange. Standing before a tall grey wall, she uttered a few odd words and what seemed to be a large portal or screen was instantly projected right out of the wall sustained in the air where she could see Adrien and Adelina Volcotrans inside their home. No other residency in the country had this surreal technology. They greeted each with a bow and mutual respect. While all three of them greeted on the doorstep of the home entrance, it almost seemed as if the ultraviolet rays of the sun became visible to the naked eye glowing with splendor and vibrant colors then gradually subsided as they entered the home. Now the million-dollar question was, who were these three folks beyond their names?

The very next day they arrived in Washington DC as they made their way to the white house accompanied by various guards. Thousands of people crowded the area including Matvey Lukenchoff and various world leaders. The stage was set for something big about to take place.

These three individuals were about to disclose crucial information to the government and everyone across the planet. As the trio made their way to the stage, everyone observed their gracious movement as if moving in slow motion that gave the appearance as if floating, but it was due to such gentle and eloquent movement of their body.

A tremendous feeling of pressure in the atmosphere filled the entire city when. These individuals stood next to each other on the stage. Just before Adrien began speaking, a huge warrior's sword materialized right in his hands out of nothing. Truly this was something unbelievable as even the US president notified the generals to be alert. Adrien lifted this weapon above their heads and lowered it before their faces, revealing their true identity unto the entire world.

It was now evident they were not entirely humans but something else not of this world, or at least partially. They grew substantially within just a few moments to over eleven feet tall with body width expanding to around three feet in diameter. Their clothing changed to black rags and chains around their bodies. flesh seemed to turn like a hornet's nest or charred rotting meat. They wore blue head hoodies, but the most horrific aspect of these beings was their "eyes" they were completely vacant as if looking into a small hole in space of passing clouds. They basically had no eyes like humans do. The two women Loretta Alkala and Adelina were not female in appearance now either.

Adrien spoke and said:

"Now you have all witnessed what we really are in our true nature. We have lived among you for thousands of years changing appearance as time evolves! We were once drowned in the sea 1963BC on another continent on this same planet, "but we have now returned to the surface returned us to the surface, and we respond to the calling; Jannes & Jambres! The creatures currently threatening your safety are commanded by us and are at our command! Stay out of our path and you may live"!

A general standing nearby asked, "where do you come from and what power do you possess to threaten us this way? We distinctly observed the weapon appear in your hands seemingly from nowhere".

One of them responded saying, "we are [the lector priests] risen from Egypt and today we are one and everywhere"!

The general glanced over at the president with a worried look on his face, but the president seemed more puzzled as to what was their agenda. He notified the military to be on high alert once more and that if they made the slightest move in aggression, to light them up with Apache helicopters hovering nearby.

That was a declaration of power but just as he began to make a statement toward this massive trio, the one believed to have been Loretta Alkala shouted in a commanding tone, "enough! We have said what we must but there is still more you do not know"!

At that moment government agents attempted to punish these huge beings for disrespecting the president but could not even get near them. They were basically neutralized and frozen in one place with what seemed to be some type of telekinetic power coming from Adelina. The general ordered all military personnel and agents to stand down and not to provoke these individuals.

The President had not yet spoken but he finally said. "you three are in the presence of the most feared military on the planet and I as leader of the free world cannot let you leave us in alarm"!

What do you want with us and what is occurring in the country of Guatemala? What is that thing or things in the jungle? Is that monster one of your creatures? Please tell us what we want to know!"

It appeared Adrien was the leader of the three; he entered a trance momentarily when that question was asked with his gaze directly forward as if concentrating. At that moment, he waved his three-fingered hands and a transparent screen with hieroglyphics appeared, displaying mysterious codes and possible locations in Guatemala. Incredibly it vividly showed the actual movement and origins of that beast. It was evident that creature was enormous with hooves instead of feet as it was clearly seen on the cast glass-like screen this being had launched before him which seemed to simply have been projected as if he had the ability to construct objects into existence.

The general standing a few yards away asked' "Mr. Volkotran, please; tell us what is that thing we are observing on your screen? It has killed off nearly half the population in that country"!

Adrien, now evident to be from outside this world or so it appeared, replied; "It is not one with us and it does not belong in your world, but it came from beneath the earth near the crust of this planet. It has lived there for thousands of years and nothing you possess can defeat it"!

At that moment these three very intriguing and strange beings simply vanished into nothing leaving a shimmer vapor behind exactly where they stood, like that which is seen protruding from the hood of a car on a hot day or from hot asphalt.

Clyde and his wife sky embraced each other lovingly as if saying God help us to each other standing in front row to this incredible spectacle with a very worried look on their faces.

Matvey Lukenchoff was seen quickly opening his computer and inserting an external USB and giving a thumbs up to several Russian officials who were present. One of the US generals told him this was not the time to conceal vital information because the entire planet is at stake.

The US president was seen having a discussion with the French prime minister beneath some trees a few hundred yards away using lots of hand gestures as if clearly afflicted.

The crowd was still leaving the secured lawn when the beast suddenly appeared among thousands of people. It simply fell from the sky but was not even observed where it came from. It was as if it just materialized as it reached the ground. It was at least twelve feet tall and very large with a mutilated body as if it went through a meat grinder and survived but the most frightening aspect of it was that its feet were turned backward and had no toes. It was the same creature from the jungles of Guatemala. On its chest area was a device that looked like an axe concealed in a holder with the handle crisping with electricity as well as huge fangs in its mouth and a machete strapped to its waste inside a holster with the scales with Mayan symbols and strange hieroglyphics charts.

At that moment the orders were given to everyone to take cover and disperse from the area and direct orders were given to the military to fire.

Hundreds of machine guns opened fire at this thing with thousands of rounds hitting their target. After about two minutes of an endless hail of bullets; it stopped allowing for the Smoke to clear.

Marine soldiers shouted; "target remains, target remains; this thing should be in pieces"!

Orders were given by the generals to four Apache helicopters hovering nearby to engage with hellfire missiles since it survived a hail of machine gun.

The president and his entire administration were wrapped away and taken to a secure location since it was beginning to look obvious that this fight is going to be a difficult one and this demonic beast is unstoppable but that is about to be known.

Apache pilots reported, "target acquired"!

"Engage engage, send that thing straight to hell"! shouted the lieutenant of one of the gunships. Multiple hellfire missiles were fired directly at the beast. It saw the missiles coming and incredibly greeted one of them with a huge, closed fist punch exploding on impact. The entire location where this demonic entity was standing went up in a great ball of fire, and when the smoke and dust had settled; this creature was clearly severely injured but not entirely down; it quickly healed itself and launched a massive counterattack because it appeared to have the ability to heal itself.

It attacked multitudes of people still in the area attempting to flee but unfortunately many did not make it out.

Bodies bathed in blood were catapulted into the air, others were being ripped to shreds.

The US president had been taken to a secured location nearby before this beast made its presence known but was still updated every few minutes. This diabolical creature then turned its attention to the military men nearby who had moments ago fired upon it

The president immediately ordered the brightest minds to quickly perform research on what this thing is and where it came from for it is clearly a major threat, not only to global stability but to the very fabric of existence itself. It seemed quite unstoppable since it withstood a powerful gunfire assault and hellfire missile strikes. This creature instantly turned itself into an incredible whirlwind of dangerous crystals as it vanished from sight.

The president and his staff quickly sent orders requesting the presence of Clyde Harper, his wife Sky and the cooperation from the Russian president to send in Matvey Lukenchoff as well. All researchers, scientists, and theologians from everywhere were being called in to assist in an effort to find where this thing came from, what it really is and how to destroy it' keeping in mind that they still had the Volkotrans to deal with and who knows what they really were, where they came from and where they had gone.

The world now had two different entities to battle, with the chances of victory looking almost impossible.

Night had settled in and no one knew where the Volkotrans and that creature had gone but what was clear was that the entire planet was in serious trouble.

The following day an eerie sound was heard coming from all corners of the planet. Scientists were called to analyze this strange and haunting sound that came with somewhat of a vibration in the chest. Clyde Harper told the government that the sound was coming from a different timeline in existence because no decibel meters stationed around the planet were picking up sound waves so to convert into electric signals, indicating the haunting echoes were not real. Clyde stated it seemed likely to him that it was intended to create distraction and fear rather than an impending danger.

At this point all the nations of the planet were at the task of unravelling what they were dealing with and where all the assaults and sounds were coming from and why. Keep in mind not only was the entire world up against a menacing diabolical indestructible beast but also a far more threatening entity; "The Volkotrans", if that was indeed a true surname.

Two days later' on a rainy Tuesday morning the French president, completely unannounced arrived in Washington DC.

The US president was surprised but delighted to welcome one of his close allies under the NATO alliance.

Be it known that whenever a foreign head of state makes his or her way to visit the US president, an announcement is usually made ahead of time, but this visit seemed a bit odd. Every head of state is always accompanied by a security team and formally greets the receiving head of state whose country is being visited but this time, the French president walked quickly toward the US president with nothing more than a light tap on the shoulder with a worried look on his face. The American president was not aware of the visit until a couple of hours before the French president landed at Dulles international airport but did receive his unannounced guest warmly as they always do.

They quickly made their way to the white house with security vehicles following behind. It appeared something was going on and the public was soon to know.

They spent extended hours locked behind closed doors along with several scholars, history experts, scientists, and theologians. Included were Matvey Lukenchoff, Clyde Harper, his wife Sky, and several NASA officials.

The French president stated, "Mr. president, we have discovered who these creatures are and where they came from but have not the least idea what they want with us all. You will not believe me when I tell you what our historical experts found out pertaining to the three beings; however, regarding the other one, the large hellish creature; sir, we don't know.

What we do now know is that they uttered the names Jannes and Jambre a few days ago during the national meeting when the confrontation occurred. Those two names Mr. president' dates to around the 13th or 14th century; some 3,500 years ago, precisely during the time of Moses. They are believed to have been powerful sorcerers who worked for pharaoh. They are mentioned in the old and in the New Testament of the bible in the book of Exodos where they challenged the prophet Moses who was a legendary figure in his time. Their names also appear in pagan Greek and roman literature.

Mr. president, these things are not of our time frame, yet they are here among us, alive and very powerful. We do not know how they re-emerged from such a long time ago and where they have been all this time.

We know nothing about why they are here and what they seek with us now, thousands of years later! That is all our experts have discovered. It is now an excessively big obligation and work to discover everything about them to protect ourselves and our nations from possible annihilation if that is what they plan to execute."

The US president, impressed by the French president's remarks, turned to Clyde Harper and asked:

"Mr. Harper what are your thoughts on this"?

Clyde Harper replied:

"Sir; it is a bit outside my expertise and highly incredible for such a thing to be possible, but we cannot rule out anything at this point. They have returned because they may be looking for something they need, and it is evident they are not entirely human and clearly, they possess supernatural elements which today are extremely rare and unknown to the highest degree.

It may be appropriate to seek religious assistance in this delicate matter. To Say we can defeat them because they are four thousand years old, would be an understatement."

No one knew how to proceed but the US president instructed to seek for the most intelligent Christian and other religious scholar to unravel the real nature of the beings.

The very next day, an Egyptian government employee decided to speak to her government regarding the three beings roaming the earth claiming she knew in detail what they are and what they want. Her name was Delylah. She was quite special in nature, portraying unique qualities, jet black hair with very deep penetrating grey eyes.

Her ancestors were descendants from kings and queens. She had been a scholar examining her people's 'history.

She also had been following the terrifying incidents that occurred beneath the Afghan ground several weeks ago as well as the horrific ordeals the Guatemalan people and surrounding territories had been going through, with the demonic beast believed to have originated from the jungles of central America, although those three huge creatures stated that it came from deep within the earth.

It had been several days since the confrontation between the beast and the US military. As for the Volkotrans, if that was truly their names had not been seen nor heard from in a while as well.

Two days later attention was brought to the Egyptian president with the news that one of its own citizens knew what was going on with the three being and perhaps what they wanted with humanity, so the president of Egypt requested to have the young lady brought into his presence immediately but less than one hour after she declared of knowing this mystery, a sonic boom was heard in all corners of the African continent. Moments later a giant dust storm engulfed the entire region from Petra to Alexandria, blotting out the sun. The Egyptian government immediately dispatched a squadron of warplanes outside the area of the dust storm to get a bigger picture of what had occurred, as well as placing its ground troops into battle and ordered everyone to be ready for a possible assault.

Layla already knew what it was, so she made her way to "Heliopolis "near the city of Cairo, the main residence of the president who was there along with his entire local administration and members of his military force. They all had an idea of who or what it was, but they were not sure if it was the Volcotrans or that monstrous beast which had confronted the US military not long ago.

Observation planes sent an unbelievable report to the government with the words; "we are in for a major fight "!

All communications to a dozen fighter jets went down completely.

They were all simply crushed in midflight. All pilots were killed instantly.

Media news started to come in. What the cameras captured was terrifying. It was the Volkotrans and they had grown immensely to over twelve feet. One, thought to be Adrien Volkotran, appeared as a giant human—much like the Nephilim described in some biblical chronicles. They were observed moving toward the cities from the direction of the hills of Mokattam out in the desert.

News cameras showed what appeared to be a stream of black or murky water being left behind them as they moved forward across the landscape. It was a scary sight to observe; however, Orders were given to fire dozens of missiles and M2 machine gun rounds at them, but all the projectiles fell to the ground midflight toward them.

The government of that country sent a request to NATO for support and the call was received. The US government was briefed instantly on what was occurring in that part of the world and it immediately sent in extra firepower and equipment along with several thousand American troops to join the retaliation in Egypt.

The United Kingdom also responded with its own backup sending in troops and jetfighters within a few hours of getting the plea for help, as well as Israel coming to the aid of its neighbor since they too were impacted by the sonic boom and the dust storm which had dissipated into the horizon.

While all this was happening, Layla was escorted by top government officials into the presence of the president of that country.

This young woman was indeed a specimen of intrigue. She was quite focused and graceful as the president greeted her even among the turmoil happening in the moment.

She spoke and said:

Sir: "what I have to say, may sound like an absurdity, but these beings existed around three thousand years ago. They worked for pharaoh as wizards and my studies on this subject are extensive. I am almost positive these creatures were directly involved in the confrontation between pharaoh and Moses Mr. president. They are immensely strong and powerful, but their power comes from evil. I know it sounds incredible, but it is true.

Jannes and Jambre were the names they have aways used, also referred to in Greek mythology. They mentioned that they were drowned in the water Mr. president; And that demonic menace from the central american jungles is referred to as an {ishtabai}, an evil spirit in the flesh, manifesting itself through the mental strength of hundreds of years of local folklore; hence, it is for long believed that mankind has unique mental abilities if discovered, similar to analyzing a problem and finding a solution. The solution is not invented but instead born; whilst, evil has a way of being attracted by negative thoughts, the mind acts as a conduit.

These things cannot be destroyed by military weapons. They will just absorb any and everything fired at them. They are spoken of in the Exodus.

I will tell you all right now; I do not know why nor how they are here, but they died thousands of years ago". Many officials were visibly trembling in fear at the incomprehensible situation.

Layla went into a room within the government compounds and took out two strange looking stones and placed them on the floor behind here and in front, then chanted what sounded like a special prayer. An official walked by and asked her what she was doing during such a critical time?

Layla replied, "we will most likely need a divine intervention to stop them".

All this incredible activity was happening in the Sahara Desert, while back in the US a rare case of illness was taking place. People were showing signs of alpha radiation. This had officials scrambling for a remedy. They knew it had to do with everything that was going on but the challenge of finding a remedy was not that simple.

This type of radiation is not significant outside of the body but if inhaled, digested or enters through a wound it can cause serious damage to any living tissue. US officials were attempting to assess the situation but were unable to save hundreds of thousands of people.

If Janes and Jambre were behind this, stopping their attack on humanity would likely be impossible.

Assaults were happening on both continents at the same time, but it was clear that the Guatemalan demonic being had disappeared. No one had seen it in several weeks while these recent attacks were being carried out. Officials were beginning to suspect the two entities were here on earth for different reasons and both being of different origins.

Matvey Lukenchoff urged world leaders to consider nuclear warheads as a last resort against the invulnerable beings, but they hesitated due to fears of global destruction. Lukenchoff argued that only such weapons might be able to defeat these creatures.

As Alexandria came under attack, Jannes and Jambre suddenly paused in deep concentration, causing the assault to halt unexpectedly and leaving everyone confused. A moment later a huge haunting growl was heard from all corners of the surrounding Mokottam hills; far off in the horizon the beast of Guatemala was approaching but this time it was not alone. It was accompanied by his friends; 4 more giant beasts looking like they had risen right out hell itself. Burnt flesh with goat horns and bright red eyes began approaching slowly gliding over the surface stopping just a few yards away from the Egyptian creatures. Face to face, two supernatural gangs about to go toe to toe or at least that is what it looked like. Jannes and Jambre, though outnumbered by two, were massive—each over twelve feet tall and heavily built. Military tanks attempted to fire but failed because They were completely disabled. All army officials were struck in awe waiting to see what would follow. It appeared to be a standoff perhaps telepathically arguing who was going to be the one to tear mankind apart. One of the members of Jannes and Jambre struck the ground with its black rod causing it to open releasing a brilliant glow of light to emerge almost like that of a projector lens. It seemed as if this light was visible gravity, attempting to suck the group of Guatemalan beasts under the ground, but it failed. Although momentarily strained, they quickly rose higher to evade the attack. Suddenly a mega squadron of American B2 bombers, F22 raptors along with dozens of Apache attack helicopters accompanied by British air power as well; appeared approaching from the west of the city of Alexandria. All military personnel cheered as powerful reinforcements arrived to support their fight against these beings. Within seconds, hundreds of American Patriot missiles and numerous British cruise missiles were launched, with ground forces firing at the same time. A massive battle between humans and supernatural forces was taking place in the Sahara Desert before the world. Powerful explosions shook the entire region. Dust and smoke blocked out the sun. A powerful electronic missile quickly struck the beings from another location, but it was unclear whether this human attack had any impact.

There were reports indicating that the electronic shot was a newly developed weapon created by a tech company called "Futureshot".

It generated a powerful static charge, far stronger than lightning, resulting in significant destruction. When it struck its target, it instantly absorbed all nearby energy, clearing the area of dust and smoke. When this happened, to the confusing sight before everyone present witnessing this incredible fight, these creatures had completely vanished. Not even a trace remained. The only thing left on the very spot where they stood was an ancient metallic scepter about six feet long standing upright balancing perfectly still with an animal head on the very top that seemed like that of a wolf. No one approached it but tv cameras were zooming in to take a close look at what it was; while the fighter jets were circling above requesting ground visual of the target, also observing the peculiar object left behind from the air. A few seconds after it also shimmered out of sight. It simply disappeared in thin air. What the entire military and people present during this confrontation did not know was that everyone who had set eyes upon that scepter would perish even if observed through camera lenses. Delylah attempted to warn against staring at the object, but the crowd noise drowned her out in speaking. She told military leaders that the scepter was very likely cursed since its owners were masters of dark magic and sorcery. After all; as much difficult as it was to believe, these very same creatures challenged the prophet moses around three thousand years ago.

The question at this point was:

Where did they go?

Officials had begun assessing all the damage on the battlefield. Many of them were in disbelief as to how such a thing could happen in the real world in modern days without a scientific explanation. The reason was that none existed.

The US president was informed of everything that had occurred and he himself was entirely confused and very much concerned.

He told his top commanders he didn't believe they were battling ghosts or demons, but his secretary of state and defense team insisted the threat was real and urgent. He was also advised to place all differences aside and unite to form a coalition and strategy with all other willing nations in efforts to neutralize the possibility of extermination. Many leaders were beginning to believe that they were not going to survive against these beings.

Since the major conflict took place, thirteen days have elapsed without any incidents or reported sightings of Jannes and Jambre entity, or the formidable creature that remains impervious to eradication.

Life was gradually returning to normal, but leaders and the military continued reconnaissance, and criminal activity was resurfacing. Following the recent war on terror, global tension remained high, with memories of its impact still evident in people's behavior. Clyde received a text from his wife explaining that Delyla, called from the Middle East, claiming to have dreams forewarning another disaster and wanted to meet them, along with Mr. Matvey Lukenchoff. Clyde told his wife that any attempt to neutralize yet another assault was welcome.

After all, even with several nations combined and heavy weaponry, they were unsuccessful in stopping the assaults.

Delylah was a unique woman with strong ties to the Israelites from much long ago. Her demeanor was light and peaceful, direct and tender but also super intelligent and intimidating due to her piercing dark eyes and jet-black hair.

Clyde and his wife ended up meeting with Delylah in Washington DC in the halls of a government building adjacent to capitol hill with Matvey Lukenchoff in tow as well as a few high-ranking officials, one of which was Allan Mateman. No one knows why he was there, but he was a government official believe it or not. He kept his attention on Delylah, but those who knew him doubted he truly valued her expertise. The look on his face was that of yearning and desire rather than the mega problem they were trying to understand and hopefully deter. Clyde Harper stood up and walked over to him and told him to immediately get rid of that ridiculous expression of constipated canine or leave the room. Mr. Mateman tried his best to compose himself but evidently, he had perhaps several demons rattling his inner peace in the form of women.

Sky begged Delylah to ignore and please excuse such an awkward and unpleasant moment while Allan Mateman exited the hall. It was around nine am when they commenced the meeting; however, fifteen minutes later several administration officials arrived to get Sky and Clyde as they apologized to Delylah for the inconvenience. They were being called by the secretary of state due to an alarming finding requiring their expertise.

Delylah watched them leave, her gaze curious and focused. Perhaps intrigued and overlooked but she was highly intelligent and very much an aristocrat. After all she was Assyrian royalty.

These repeated assaults were happening in late summer and early fall of 2000, but the objective predates this time frame, perhaps by hundreds if not thousands of years because no one knows how long it had been since these beings had been around pretending to be humans.

Eight days later, just before Halloween a family from Kingman Arizona was on the way to Rosarito Mexico for vacation. The sun had just disappeared behind the hills with a cool breeze blowing through the trees and brushes on the side of the road. The thermometer in their vehicle stated it was seventy-three degrees outside with a little over half a tank of fuel left before they would need to stop at a roadside gas station. At exactly ten twenty-two pm, no more than twenty-five yards ahead just outside the illuminated path of vision from the vehicle's headlamps stood a figure dressed in black garments with what appeared to be a dark coat from the eighteenth century with shoulder length hair covering its facial features. The minivan family abruptly stopped, caught in suspense.

It appeared to be a man, but when the vehicles high beam lights were activated, those in the vehicle could not believe what they saw. The man was floating about three feet off the ground lifting its head to the heavens in the darkness of the night. A little boy inside the van with very good eyesight screamed out; "Dad, Mom it has fangs like a dog and white eyes; look:

There are more of them in the woods!"

When the van driver aimed his flashlight beam at the roadside trees, it revealed three more floating creatures motionless above the forest floor. Just staring at the family inside the minivan who were already panicking.

What are those things one member of the family asked?

A teenager in the rear seat said they were most likely extraterrestrials but that was unlikely because they probably did not have the ability to simply float and glide through the air.

That family never made it to the border. In fact, they did not even make it to the next town.

Two Days later their minivan was fond in a large open savannah much smaller than its regular size completely smashed in from all sides. It looked as if it was compressed, making it appear smaller.

The FBI were called in along with Sky Harper. With no witness, the task at hand to unravel what occurred to this family was a difficult one but Sky was already suspecting it could be related to what had been happening all over the globe with Jannes and Jambre and that indestructible beast.

This time it was different because it was quite clear those dark shadow creatures were new in the area and never seen before, although no one knew about them except for the missing family, but they were gone; one thing was certain:

No earthly force could have done to that minivan what was done to it without heavy machinery leading investigators to believe that this family on their way to a vacation had an encounter with a reconning force.

The entire location where the disappearance of these people had occurred was secured and restricted by law enforcement and the FBI.

Matvey Lukenchoff arrived hours later and spoke with Sky Harper about the situation. Notably, Clyde Harper, Sky's spouse, had not yet become involved in this recent incident.

Agents could be seen taking samples and fingerprints but with a confused expression on their faces.

One of them could be heard saying to another that he strongly believes that the missing family was abducted but that he could not understand why no prints nor footsteps were left behind, let alone, no signs of a struggle. Not even a blood stain nor belongings because everything was still on location.

The lead FBI agent walked over to Sky and asked her where Clyde was and she stated that he was in Egypt finalizing reports on the terrifying incident in the Saharah desert needing to be presented to NATO, regarding a potential manhunt and assault on "Jannes and Jambre" and that demonic creature.

This recent incident occurred around eleven pm and it was now nine am, but the wooded area made it look as if it was still six am due to tall trees.

There were precisely nine officials present at the location.

Harper, Lukenchoff, Mateman, two sheriff deputies and four other agents.

All of them climbed into a brand new, robust Chevy Suburban with deeply tinted windows and left for the city, carrying circumstantial evidence. But soon after merging onto Highway Ninety-Five between Bullhead City and Interstate Forty, they noticed that the whole landscape surrounding them had transformed.

The highway miles noted on the sides of the road was now in roman numerals and trees to the side seemed much taller when they were no more than twenty feet tall; furthermore, these new trees do not grow in dry desert regions.

These agents inside their vehicle were now alarmed and completely confused since not even their training could help them.

It was as if they were unwillingly transported into a different dimension parallel to our own.

At that moment the highway itself appeared to change. A simmering heat originated out of nowhere causing the tires on the vehicle to explode on the asphalt. Steam could be seen rising out of the ground all around them.

Moments later the entire highway ninety-five was on fire with flames rising about ten feet into the air causing the agents inside to quickly exit and seek safety or their suburban would be incinerated. Out of the fire in the middle of the highway these creatures came gliding. There were seven beings whose feet did not touch the ground. They wore hoods making them look like witches with long ragged cloaks.

Face to face with government agents in broad daylight.

The agents drew guns, some with rifles, but these creatures did not seem moved whatsoever by weapons; perhaps, they did not even know or recognize what a gun was. One of the agents shouted, "guys, they have no shadow, look"!

Sure enough, these beings were not casting a shadow on the ground even with the sun shining brightly.

Their faces could not be seen because their hood and dark cloaks covered them, but they were floating about two feet above the ground with what appeared to be electricity at the fingertips. These agents were trapped in a different reality or dimension parallel with our own and they were in very serious trouble.

No one on site could figure out what these things were but one thing was evident.

They were not human.

In the blink of an eye, one of these things made a sweeping motion with its right hand and simply erased the agents along with their guns in hand.

Even the suburban parked in the middle of the highway was basically vanquished into nonexistence. The agents did not even have time to fire a shot and if they did, that shot would have been fired in the afterlife because not even their shoes were left behind. It was as if they were never there. At that moment everything returned to normal, the landscape remolded itself to its original position.

Several agents along with Sky Harper and Allan Mateman were either dead or sent off to another world.

This was going to be devasting news for Clyde Harper, sky's husband and his two young children. Sky was a brunette agent with light grey eyes and an energy to solving mysteries for the US government.

A distress signal was sent just before the agents were eliminated and the president was notified about members of his administration killed in action while investigating the disappearance of a family on a vacation trip.

The family who was most likely killed on that highway were Kate and Samuel Gruber with their children, a normal American family who worked in healthcare with their kids still in high school.

Now at this point official members of the government were killed and the heads of state, not only from the US but from most of NATO allies were informed that civilians in America were attacked and slain without a trace.

There was no evidence of murder, yet most government agencies had already classified it as a crime.

Clyde Harper was enroute back to his home state of California to spend some time with his family. He had purchased tickets for a cruise on a Norwegian ship up the coast of Alaska, but when his plane landed at LAX international airport, several FBI agents and military personnel greeted him with the most terrible news that his wife Sky had been killed.

Clyde Harper fell to his knees at that moment with terrible agony and tears flowing like a river from his eyes.

He vowed with intense visible anger as he clutched his fists driving them onto the tarmac, "I will murder whoever did this, I swear I will take you out, he yelled out.

Several days later a funeral was held for Sky and the other members of the government even without the bodies, but the investigation was on, with all firing cylinders. Helicopters could be seen flying over the scenes where the incident took place almost a week later

Lukenchoff being a highly intelligent Russian official who had teamed up with several other bright minds brought in what he called a "triumphant scanner" which he claimed to have the ability to detect invisible entities such as abstract energies, spirits, pulses, emp bursts and perhaps more of the unseen.

The device was unable to capture anything except heat signatures from a few animals inside the forest.

Meanwhile, Clyde Harper was at home in the suburbs of Los Angeles California which was his home state with his two teenage children refusing to answer his telephone; after all, his suffering was not for the faint of heart. No one knew what became of him in several days since Sky had been gone but anyone can agree that he needed to be as close to the kids as possible attempting to fill in that empty space left by his beloved wife.

weeks had gone by, and everything seemed to have returned to normal, but officials and world leaders were still on alert of any abnormality across the globe because they knew those beings were still roaming the earth somewhere, perhaps in the most remote parts of the planet.

A month later, Clyde Harper went jogging in his California suburb, wearing a beanie, sweatpants, and a white sweater with a Bengal tiger logo.

As soon as he exited his driveway onto the surface street; there stood Delylah on the curb leaning on a gorgeous 2021 Cadillac CTS; folding in what appeared to be weapons located on the lower sides making it look like it had jet wings hidden beneath the body extending outward from its sides.

It was a state or the art vehicle decked out with its own armor and aerodynamics.

Clyde walked up to her and stood there with an empty gaze and hands on his hips. A cool wind blew as they both stood facing each other when out of nowhere Delylah gave him a tight hug and told him that she felt the sorrow of him losing his wife Sky and that she felt her duty was to comfort a great colleague in great pain as well as to assist him in any needs he may have, since Sky herself told her that her pride and joy was her husband and her children to always be happy.

She felt that Sky would have appreciated someone being there for her family since she had passed.

Clyde told her; "nice wheels"!

She replied, "reminds me who I am"!

"How have you been D"?

said Clyde!

she replied, "busy, let's talk over coffee"!

They both stepped into that amazing vehicle and drove off like a lightning strike.

While they sat at a local eatery, a group of armed men entered with rifles drawn, yelling to get down on the floor but none was wearing mask which means they were certain regarding their bravery. Sending a message to everyone that they were untouchable with or without masks.

They immediately shot a cashier dead in the forehead without even requesting money, then they shot a construction worker on his morning break point blank right in the face.

The wound was so severe that his entire left cheek was hanging by shredded flesh only. The rest did as they were told to get on the floor. There were around twelve to fifteen persons dining but two were killed.

Clyde and Delylah were in a booth on the far corner of the diner and were the only ones to ignore the orders of these hard-core criminals.

Clyde stood up from his chair and as he did, he said to Delylah; "these are the ones those damn creatures should have erased from the face of the earth"!

He walked slowly toward the attackers without the least amount of fear and a huge rifle pointed at his forehead, but in less than two seconds that assailant was on his back beaten down by Clyde.

Delylah got up quickly as well and jumped into action with a thundering round house kick from her Dr. Marten boots hitting two assailants simultaneously. Clyde approached the final assailant who was unable to discharge his weapon before being incapacitated by two rapid and skillful strikes that demonstrated Clyde's advanced martial arts proficiency.

The only thing visible on his last takedown was his fingers on both hands extended out in front of him like the claws of a tiger.

Unbelievable beatdown even against weapons.

All the assailants were on the floor yelling in pain. Two of the diner patrons stated in a loud voice that one of the criminals had his collar bone exposed with a bloody neck. Paramedics were called in since clearly this gang of thieves were severely injured.

Another had a boot heel stuck in his cheekbone bleeding profusely.

The entire dinner had turned into a battleground with several definite casualties since it's unlikely one of them will survive. It did seem that Clyde Harper ripped out the carotid artery causing heavy bleeding on one of them as well as blood on his hands. That's the reason when the fight was over, his hands were in the form of a tiger's claw.

The youngest of the assailants even peed in his pants due to the gruesome sight of his friends being so badly beaten. He got up off the floor limping on one leg, holding his lower back. The others were loaded onto stretchers and taken to the emergency room, quite possibly halfway dead.

One thing was certain; Clyde and Delylah were masters in hand combat with such incredible speed and smooth skills.

They both gave each other a hug. Delylah told him she was unaware of his combat skills. Clyde told her he acquired it living in Thailand and Philippines long ago and never forgotten it.

They both got into Delylah's fancy vehicle and drove away like a shooting star with a thundering roar.

The fourth of July was only 2 days away and preparations for celebrations were ongoing. Fireworks could be seen exploding everywhere in many cities but in Peru, something horrific was beginning to take place in the town of [Cusco]not far from the citadel of [Machu Picchu].

The giant body of a creature towering over fifteen feet tall standing at the base of this citadel looking like a medieval warrior with a silver helmet and a twelve-foot-tall spear in its left hand guarded by the very same beings responsible for the killings of Sky and her team as well as an American family on route to a vacation.

In the middle east another of these creatures stood tall on the coast of the city of Alexandria in Egypt, but was unguarded; however, this one was raising alarm bells everywhere because it had basically four tornados of black smoke swirling all around him rising over a thousand feet in the air, with head tilted down toward the ground.

Its face was hidden by shrouds of linen and hair, also holding a scepter in its right hand.

People were gathering to observe this thing, and many were stating that it is a live being because they had seen it moved its head.

This one in the middle east was alone while the other in [Cusco, Peru] had its guardians.

Notifications were going out to all corners of the planet that something ominous was about to occur. The US president being the leader of the free world held a press conference stating that he is even willing to deploy nuclear warheads if these beings decide to act against humanity.

This day was about to be marked as historical because what was about to occur would bring all of humanity to its knees.

It was a Monday morning in Peru, while the United States was about to celebrate its independence.

With over a thousand people gathered near the foothills of [Machu Pichu], at exactly twelve noon, that giant being came into motion.

This thing raised its left arm with that huge scepter in its grasp and drove it into the ground causing a tremendous shockwave across the region shattering huge chunks off the mountain near where it stood; furthermore, causing tremendous rockslides.

Everyone fled in panic, while those responsible for previous disappearances quickly surrounded the thousand onlookers, who anxiously watched the strange activity unfold.

Incredibly, ancient keepers of the Peruvian mountains swung down the mountainside by the hundreds on "Peruvian pepper trees" armed with strange weapons for they knew these beings were about to cause destruction.

All were present, but mere seconds afterward, the seven floating beings launched an assault on more than a thousand human beings.

People were basically ripped apart from the inside out by what appeared to be kinetic energy. No one knew what those beings were, but they were obviously out to exterminate humanity. As for the twenty-foot beings. They were more like statutes able to move but were mostly immobile up to this point.

The entire foothills of "Machu Picchu" looked like a killing field with destroyed bodies lying everywhere and organs basically ripped out of the body.

Not one person was even touched. This was done entirely by a power no one could stop and counter.

Telephone calls were being made in desperation to law enforcement of Peru as well as officials of the government, but help was too late.

When assistance arrived, one thousand three hundred and sixty-three people were dead. Those dark humanoid beings were gone and so was the giant beast.

The Peruvian president urgently contacted the US president on a secure line, reporting a mass killing at a world wonder base carried out by inhuman perpetrators.

Moments later, on the shores of Alexandria Egypt, the other giant creature lifted its head. Its eyes were bright yellow with a long beard and a hood over its head. It raised its staff and blasted off into the air leaving a shockwave behind causing small waves on the ocean as well as a large crater where it stood. These things were truly massive and dangerous. It was clear they possessed the power to eliminate an entire army if they desired.

That very same afternoon the US president called an emergency cabinet meeting in the situation room. Several dozens of top officials were called in to participate with many media outlets.

Generals from all over the country and abroad were called as well, in great haste. This was a dire situation because Norad was tracking multiple unidentified objects circling above just outside the Karman line which is at the beginning of space located about sixty-two miles from the surface of the earth.

The president was on the phone lines as well with other leaders across the world since he was advised by the secretary of state and the pentagon that it may be wise to be in alliance with not just friendly allies but with everyone.

The fight that was on the way left no room for differences while attempting to battle these unworldly creatures as we all have seen what they are capable of.

One of the cabinet officials asked what about the Volkotrans and the beast of central American jungle. Another replied that it was quite likely the giant beings were from a different gang and with different objectives.

Another official responded saying, "Gang?

These things are more like killing machines".

The Russian president was the first to respond to the US president as well as the United Kingdom and French president.

Keep in mind all of this was happening prior to the war on terror away from most of the public but indeed happening. Some may not care to admit that the entire war on terror and later conflicts had something to do with the present occurrence and an even larger menace which CIA and FBI officials already suspected was coming but refused to notify everyone in efforts to prevent mass hysteria as one can expect; however, a threat in which mankind has absolutely no control over is sure to mature and become evident in its own due time and nature.

Consider that there is a great difference between something impossible and something that has simply not yet happened.

At exactly two o'clock pm eastern time, the earth beneath Washington DC shook violently causing several establishments to crumble. Even the white house was rattled with minor damage.

A strong wind picked up, and a loud boom was heard in the skies above the city.

It was the giant beings arriving where it all began with the Volkotrans in the heart of the US capital. One floated above the pentagon and the other above the white house and incredibly a third one arrived directly over the capitol hill building. They simply floated effortlessly with their long shawls and black colored cloaks hanging down on their sides like Egyptian warlords with bright yellow eyes. Truly an unbelievable sight to behold.

Hundreds of people were coming out to observe the commotion dawning with such large beings not only over Washington but on the planet itself as for such a thing had never occurred on earth.

As officials and military generals gathered outside, they immediately notified the president that it was the Volkotarans but much larger than they were before. It was evident that they had evolved throughout the weeks gone by. Within fifteen minutes large crowds gathered in the thousands. The president asked if the other smaller ones were also present outside as well. The president summoned for the presence of Clyde and Delylah since they were the most indicated to possibly communicate and find out exactly what these things wanted and give it to them so they can return to the depts of hell, where they came from, or back to the darkest reaches of the red sea out of which they apparently rose from.

It took about forty-five minutes for them to arrive, and Clyde stood nearby staring at one of them with intense hatred but could not reach them since they were floating about ten feet above the buildings nearby.

All three of them finally united on the grounds in front of the state capitol. When they landed, their feet had six toes but were far larger than a human foot. They appeared not to wear shoes but rather a rubber like gear with openings for the toes.

One of them began to speak in a vibrating voice with steam or vapor coming out of its mouth behind the words and it was July, just one day before the birth of America.

"We are Jannes and Jambre, we are one tenfold. We are one with leviathan and we come from its home.

We are one with our Pharaoh!

Bring us the one you call president. Should you refuse, he is already dead!

Bring us your kings and queens! Bring before us your most ruthless rulers and religious mediocre scholars because they too will come to know us well!

Bring before us the one from the east as well and he too will succumb in our presence.

And now I say to you putrid souls of this forsaken world; bring us Israel for this time we will finish them.

This time, "Moses" is not here to save them, and all of you sinners of the America, not even your fiery weapons can defeat us"!

Everyone was struck in awe and shattering fear. some elderly people were beginning to faint and wet themselves in quivering nervous breakdown. news and law enforcement helicopters as well as armed Apache were hovering nearby ready to fire.

Tanks were also in route to the incredible activity unfolding on the Capitol Hill grounds.

The US president was being brought forth by his guards of the secret services but before he reached the location of these giant Volkotrans, one of them motioned its huge right arm and snarled its large teeth at the news helicopters and simply obliterated four of them circling above. There was not even an explosion. Those choppers were simply erased from the air in front of every eye.

The president was now standing face to face with these beings, although he had to look up to them as they made everyone appear like midgets in comparison. Delylah and Clyde Harper were right next to the president as well as his security team. His secretary of defense by the name of Jason Newman was also with him and several respected Generals. Word was going out that the Russian president, the United Kingdom and French president were airborne toward Washington DC.

Just imagining the president of Russia in Washington DC was deeply strange and abnormal but this was not the time for differences.

Clyde Harper asked angrily, "where are those cowards who killed my wife on that highway several months ago? Why are they not here? Who are they?"

One of the giant creatures focused intensely on Clyde, stretched out its huge arm clenching Clyde by the neck without touching him, suspending him several feet above the ground, basically squeezing the life right out of him. Not even his lethal skills could save him until the president yelled, "stop! Spare his life and I will cooperate with you!"

At that moment Clyde was released and dropped to the ground.

People were now in panic with one exception: Delylah.

She was calm all along but keenly observing these beings with every word they uttered and every movement they made.

Delylah stepped forward and cried out, "I know who you are and where you come from but tell us sorcerers of Pharaoh, you were drowned in the sea along with all your kind thousands of years ago. What is it you now seek and how did you survive the wrath of [Moses] and the almighty God?

Why punish and kill humanity after so long"?

At that moment one of them once again used kinetic power by simply extending the arm and lifting Delylah a few feet above ground like what they did with Clyde bringing her closer to them but without force or injuring her.

They observed her with peculiarity inches away from their face and said, "yes, you are a descendant of them, I can smell it in your blood, but you too will perish today! YOU HEAR ME SHADDAI! ANOINTED ONE! I INVOKE YOU {METATRON}! COME DOWN FROM YOUR LOFTY DOMAIN CHOSEN ONE AND ANSWER TO OUR BATTLE COMMAND"!

Delylah was suddenly released and said in her own voice, "you are calling him to confront him while using us as bait! You are calling {Metatron} with intentions to kill him using us as valid reason for his appearance"!

One of the creatures replied, "indeed! We waited for all this time in that abyss for this moment to avenge our people's demise but not even in the blackness of that watery grave could the power of darkness be extinguished!"

Delylah immediately informed the president and other officials of what the entire ordeal was about.

"Mr. president, they want to face {the prince of presence} who was partially responsible for the eradication of pharaohs army over three thousand years ago when his holiness [Moses] with the assistance of the beloved heavenly father parted the red sea swallowing all of them at once! Somehow these three did not drown and now they seek revenge against the great [Shaddai] who [Metatron] is!"

A general standing there while staring at the beings who stood several yards away asked Delylah,

"who is this {Metatron}, where is he and why do they want vengeance against him when it was [Moses] who eliminated them or at the least, he thought he did because here we have Godzilla and king Kong along with their friend big foot, thinking they own our planet taking lives left and right, trying to resurrect a fight everyone on earth believed had ended Millenia's even before our lord "the anointed one Of Nazareth" was born"?

Before Delyla could respond, the president was informed that the Russian president had landed and the French president along with the United Kingdom prime minister was less than thirty minutes from landing but in a nontraditional way; the Russian president arrived in a c17 air carrier used to transport military equipment filled with high tech weapons and tanks. An unprecedented event occurred in America, but this was not the time for conflict with each other; humanity faces a global threat from ancient forces beyond our understanding, and provoking the mysterious entity known as {Metatron} could end any hope of survival.

A few moments later, none other than the Russian president entered the capitol front lawn followed by the French leader with the United Kingdom prime minister on his way to confront these beings along with the Americans, this was a classic situation where mankind shows its resilience and proving to any intruder regardless how strong they are that we will not perish without a fight.

As Delylah attempted to speak to government leaders on what she knows, the demonic creature from the jungles of central America also made its presence known with a thundering arrival atop a nearby building destroying part of it, with its own shockwave on arrival.

This time, it had a [Tzute] which ancient Mayan priests and Greeks wore on the head signifying strength reaching the shoulder.

Its burnt beehive looking flesh released a stench of gun powder when close, which many believed to be the scent of the devil himself; however, that theology has no fundamental certainty since no one has ever seen it.

Delyla yelled out to one of them, "who were the hooded beings responsible for the attacks on the California highway where our dear friend and colleague perished"?

"They were created by us and manipulated at will executing our desires cleansing this wretched world of sin! They no longer are needed; therefore, they were returned to the darkness of their sarcophagus.

They were already dead", replied Jannice and Jambre.

The tremendous hatred could be seen on Clyde's face clenching his fist, but he knew well he was powerless to inflict vengeance on these giant creatures.

The US president ordered on sight to ready all warheads but while he gave those orders, these beings practically knew what was intended and stated, "you are powerless earth leader, even with destructive weaponry you possess, you could never prevail"!

The Russian president could be seen quite shaken while observing the might and power standing before his eyes but tried his best to obscure his concern.

France asked; "what can we all do for you to leave our world without hurting anyone else"?

"CALL UPON YOUR SPIRITUAL LEADERS AND PROPHETS", was the reply in a strong, thundering and scolding tone.

It was indeed something unbelievable seeing these indestructible and intimidating creatures along with the demonic beast united against the entire planet and all its arsenal.

A few moments later, almost a dozen F35 raptors appeared on the horizon along with what seemed to be a type of new technology resembling a diamond shape craft with no windows nor thrusters, came into focus immediately behind the raptors approaching from the east of the DC area. A massive showdown was about to commence, and everyone took cover under buildings expecting rockets and missiles to be fired but nothing happened. These fighters-jets maintained a distance awaiting command from the president and generals. France and yes even Russia noted that they too have fighter jets armed to the teeth ready on command should the US president make the request.

The beast from the jungles kept standing atop a building nearby with growls which could be heard everywhere when suddenly it had vanished from sight as if it was never there, then reappeared standing right next to Jannice and Jambre on the ground before multitudes of people.

The face-off was truly incredible between several superpower countries and four indestructible large off-planet beings, resurrected apparently thousands of years ago. They evidently were accustomed to war and confrontations invoking something or someone named "Shaddai" or "Metatron" whom no one truly knows about, although Delylah have shed some light on this entity but far insufficient background.

The media began reporting a few moments later that the British prime minister and his entire security team had landed and arriving on site shortly.

At that moment, Delylah, who was standing behind leaders and security forces including generals, decided to walk out from in between everyone with her jet-black hair lusciously bouncing and blowing in the breeze in the nation's capital.

With an intense focus forward toward these giant creatures just across the lawn, in an immobile stand waiting for the one called' Shaddai or Metatron. Everyone was silent as she made her way toward them and uttered:

"I am a descendant of the people of Israel! I am a descendant of Moses and he who is the prince of presence for I know who you are, you wretched henchmen of the devil! You cannot defeat him because the one sitting on the throne of the most high has given him power you can never overcome!"

Immediately after that statement, two of these giant beasts opened their arms and a great whirlwind started, violently uprooting even the very grass off the lawn getting caught up into the circulating windstorm. Three limbs cracking from trees getting thrown across the street nearby with everyone running for cover, but the president stood his grounds along with his security team. Fighter jets fired at the target with heat seeking missiles, but the missiles were destroyed midair in route toward them turning into tiny, shredded metal. The Guatemalan demonic creature discharged what appeared to be a form of photon particle directly into the crowd of people numbering several thousand including the Russian and French president. All of them were blasted with deadly beams of light which came out directly from that creature's eyes.

Delylah was lifted about ten feet of the ground kinetically and brought face to face with these hellacious murderous beings, basically being stripped of her clothing and slowly her very own flesh was beginning to peel off her body.

Immediately following this direct attack on Delylah and everyone else in modern day America, something chilling began to occur.

All of Washington DC suddenly darkened; covered not by clouds but by an extremely large object which suddenly appeared about one thousand feet overhead. Military stations across the country were conveying messages that it covered the entire state including large parts of the northeast region out to the eastern seaboard. A sudden elevation in temperature was also felt and reported. A temperature spike of thirty-five degrees occurred in less than two minutes.

A strange sound of haunting synchronized and thundering harmonica could be heard all across the entire region when suddenly, the heavens opened up with a flash of light more potent than the sun itself splitting right through to the ground toasting the earth as it made ground contact leaving it black dirt, but nothing could be seen as of yet up in the heavens but something unbelievable was happening because even the creatures were looking up with eagerness and anger as a new phenomenon began to occur while in the midst of several.

Delylah was immediately released to the ground half naked with burnt injuries on her arms and around her neck area.

The skies seemed to be on fire over a vast swat of the eastern region.

Something truly shocking and incredible was occurring.

The president along with French and Russian leaders were covered and carried away by security officials under a large terrace of the capitol building while an intense vibration and an unknown heat in the air arose out of nowhere.

The four giant beasts standing nearby did not faze but did stagger a few steps back due to the happenings and vibration.

It felt like standing inches away from a powerful bass speaker blasting out loud by thousands of amps. The vibration could be felt deep in the chest almost pushing against you.

The president and the other leaders had Delylah brought out of the lawn area and into their presence to be treated for her burns and questioned about what she may know was taking place.

The high-tech military fighter jets attempted to fire MB1 Starcam missiles, a new development in the military arsenal but against these beings they were ineffective.

The entire state of Washington was under a cataclysmic event with a frightening occurrence on the ground and in the heavens above.

The heat radiating from above toward ground was shattering and unbelievable.

Fighter jets F18 standing by on firing command began reporting that the entire eastern section of the country was obscured under a large, dark and destructive reddish cumulous cloud but without thunderstorm as radar systems were not picking up any weather systems in the area, nor the cloud phenomena currently occurring. At the same time Norad, a government institution system responsible for defense was reporting a gigantic object just outside the earth's atmosphere about two hundred miles up.

In a shattering instant a giant spear at least twenty feet long fell through the clouds from high above burying itself straight into the ground through solid concrete digging a huge hole. The very top had a crown like emblem which activated on its own, suddenly launching several metallic energized brilliantly lit needle-like object about sixteen inches long straight at the giants. They were blasted on the forehead and chest area pushing them about fifty yards through several trees and into the ground with tremendous force. Incredibly those objects retracted from the target and returned faster than the speed of light back to the crown shaped object sitting on the head of the spear still buried in the shattered ground, but no one could see who launched it; however, it did come from the heavens above which was indeed a frightening sight to behold.

The skies appeared to be in flames glowing bright red then changing to brilliant yellow gold.

Norad was sending warnings that a very large object was hovering about one hundred and ninety miles above the ground covering the entire eastern half of the continental US, but radars could not distinguish what it was.

The creature from the central American jungle seemed hesitant but Growled toward the skies above as if issuing a challenge to whatever was up there.

Out of nowhere a sudden beam of radiant energy photon hit that beast straight out of the heavens blasting it into oblivion. There was no explosion or damage on the ground. The only thing heard was a thundering warping sound when it made contact. This creature was large in stature, almost thirteen feet tall and wide in body, around four feet but even though it was that large, he was no match for whatever took him out.

The Jannice and Jambre rose from the rubble on the ground in an upright position uninjured as if pulled straight up by an invisible chord and unbelievably simply blasted off into the heavens in a massive hunt for whatever was up there. Keep in mind, these things had many abilities, and flight was clearly one of them.

All the people nearby watching in suspense and shock around the state capitol were crying out, "WHAT IN THE WORLD IS HAPPENING? WHERE IS OUR MILITARY? CAN'T YOU ALL SEE WE ARE UNDER ATTACK!"

Clyde Harper told officials that he did not know what was going on, but it is something they cannot control. His kids Chess and Lark shouted out, "wow that was awesome dad!"

The president told the Russian and French leaders that it appeared that whoever or whatever was up above in the atmosphere was called upon.

Delylah confirmed that statement saying, "yes, these beings were the workers of pharaoh, thousands of years ago and they are here for vengeance using mankind as a motivation to call on him. He is the prince of presence Because he represents "The highest, the almighty God and creator" who assisted Moses in killing their people in the red sea Mr. president. The one who has now arrived in our realm is Metatron"!

The French president asked Delylah, "what is this Metatron prince, who is he?"

Delylah replied, "he is enormous sir! His body is very heavy, and his eyes are brighter than a gamma ray. In his true form, he is even bigger than the planet. Nothing can stop him because the power of the creator stands with him and is in him. He goes by many names but primarily is known as Metatron who is mentioned in very ancient non-canonical texts in the scriptures and believe it or not Mr. president, he is believed to be "the great Shaddai" or Enoch.

Some in orthodox Jewish beliefs, state that the "prince of presence" is the mortal Enoch before the Lord snatched him up and took him to heaven without tasting the bitter cup of death, due to his obedience and perfect life he led amidst chaos and perdition during the time of the Nephilim giants, later transformed into this mighty being by God himself"!

Government officials and generals standing there looking at the phenomena still occurring in the heavens said in a humorous way that they did not use to believe in the easter bunny but now they do.

We could say that it appeared that the whole world has turned upside down with world leaders not knowing what to do.

The US president asked where they had gone? Generals were on their comms devices requesting for NASA and the air force to stand vigilant and ready to defend whatever can be defended; although they all agreed that it is quite possible the world may not survive an all-out assault from these otherworldly beings. Delylah was basically saved by this Metatron celestial being because he made his arrival felt and known precisely when those giant beings were about to eliminate her.

NASA sent a report to the defense department and the pentagon that no device they possess can define what is stationed outside the Karman line, which is considered where space begins, sixty-two miles above the earth's surface. Norad was only picking up a giant patch of illumination, similar to a flame of fire which could explain the sudden high levels of heat felt around the world.

Delylah responded to the president's earlier question as to where they may have gone.

"Mr. president, please rest assured that Metatron is not here to hurt or destroy us and never will he. He represents our heavenly creator, all powerful and omnipotent. He is now here because he was invoked. Had he not come, the entire planet would succumb to those giant beasts, but it appears the jungle demon has been killed. According to some scriptures, he is even stronger than the arch angel Michael.

I believe he did not want to Cause destruction in this city; therefore, he lured off the Egyptian witches to another place"!

Clyde Harper hugged Delylah in relief of what had just occurred. It even appeared that the two of them were beginning to have feelings for one another since the passing of Sky, although only a month or two had gone by, but taking into consideration, the loss of a spouse can leave a very big empty space, especially after many years of holy union.

Those mighty beings were gone but most likely only out of the area because the entire skies still looked as if a gigantic tornado was occurring above without reaching the ground.

The high levels of heat had vanished, and everything seemed to have returned to normal; however, rumbles of thunder could be heard overhead as if a massive thunderstorm was on its way, but that was not the case. the leaders of the earth all called an emergency summit in Amsterdam Netherlands' several days later in the wake of what had recently happened.

Several days had passed and no signs of what had occurred remained. The anomaly in the skies above had disappeared and it was quite possible the threats were gone, at least, for now. A few days later Some people of rural farmlands near the Ukrainian border with Poland reported seeing a very large shining winged creature towering over trees with eyes like a bright light bulb seen caring for the animals out in the fields but no confirmation on which one of them it was; hence, there were several of them roaming the earth now.

Delylah was living in Cairo lately but had recently relocated to New York city due to everything that was going on and had developed special feelings toward Clyde and his kids who ended up without their mom in recent attacks.

The day had arrived for the summit with most leaders of the world on their way including the president of Guatemala, Brazil and Mexico. Several NASA personnel were scheduled to be present as well should questions of scientific nature arise which was sure to happen. The planet was calm for the time being with no recent threat or renewed attacks; however, many citizens and senators were asking question in great intrigue as to who Metatron is and why he cannot be seen, but there were more questions than answers because it is quite probable that not even NASA knew the nature of these powerful beings, since they are far more affiliated with the bible and ancient Christianity rather than scientific issues.

Many jetliners were flying across the globe on this day. It was a bright and partly cloudy September day when all leaders boarded their aircraft to the Netherlands. Militaries from across the planet were uniting forming one single coalition. C17 tankers were landing in Amsterdam along with massive submarines stationed just off the coast. This was the first time in history that all the militaries of the nation's once enemies decided to consolidate power in order to stand against what had been occurring; nonetheless, they had seen what those beings were capable of withstanding missiles and machine gun fire with ease. the Americans were still in rout to the summit but the firepower they were towing along with the president was unbelievable. More than one hundred fighter jets were accompanying air force one. Several aircraft were evidently state-of-the-art new technology. Hardly seen to be of this world as well as air tankers carrying dozens and dozens of tanks touching down in Amsterdam. Russia also touched down in several massive planes loaded with insane fire power as well. Some of their missiles were the late Oreshnik. Suddenly, a large semi-truck with a towing platform arrived at the tarmac and hanger area where equipment was being hauled out of the large aircraft.

What appeared to be a strange object about the size of a car was situated on top of the flatbed truck with raw lightning flashes of electricity emanating from it. It seemed to be a prototype weapon or perhaps some type of generator.

All of this was being done in efforts to secure and safeguard all these world leaders; however, we have seen what these huge beings were capable of. Unbelievably, whatever was floating in the skies above Washington obliterated the jungle beast with one single blast but the most powerful remained: Jannice and Jambre.

The day was a blistery September morning, sunny and a bit windy with some clouds from time to time passing by, above the city of Amsterdam. Most leaders from ninety-six countries had already arrived.

The US president finally made touchdown in air force one. He was being escorted by heavily armed guards which did not resemble the secret service.

These folks looked more like assassins in armored battle gear rather than casual regular protection; although, it is quite likely not even these warlords would be much protection should those creatures decide to attack.

The Russian president greeted everyone as well as the United States president along with his executive team who were heard engaging with Russian scientists and officials regarding the electronic weapon created out of direct raw power instead of alternate.

The Russians stated that the weapon was manufactured out of carbon atoms called "graphene" two hundred times stronger than steel while its interior conductors and capacitors made of copper and aluminum can safely conduct lightening electricity and channel that same energy through a cannon to be attached. That blast can carry energy of fifty thousand degrees Fahrenheit which is five times hotter than the surface of the sun.

Their intent is to roast those giant beings alive should they show up once again along with insane firepower. All in attempt to save mankind from what could be a full extermination.

Every leader along with news cameras and reporters numbering in the hundreds; perhaps even up to a thousand from across the globe were gathered in an open coastal location called Zandvoort' off the coast of the North Sea not far from Amsterdam.

It was a huge open stadium where basically leaders from the entire globe were about to speak to the entire planet and let humanity know what has been happening and how they plan to counter any further attack.

Not long after all these leaders were gathered along with thousands of people in attendance at what was being called "address to mankind", precisely the moment the Italian prime minister was stepping down from the podium, no military radar system could detect what appeared far off on the horizon of the North Sea. About two miles away

The ancient Egyptian sorcerers known as Jannice and Jambre were returning perhaps to finish off humanity.

They appeared as radiating heat above the water. Like a strong vapor causing the sea water below to appear as if it was evaporating. Their presence even from couple miles away was causing the ground to crack lightly and groan as if the earth itself was in pain. The vapor of water could be seen as if it was sucking out sea water and casting it miles into the air above.

They all floated in perfect synchronization about ten to fifteen-feet apart. Their bodies occupied a wide area roughly about eight feet in width. They were huge in physique as well as being very tall with ragged attire and what is called a "khepresh" or "war crown" on the head.

Their faces were terrifying with eyes that looked like space itself. Empty pocket holes with nothing but rapidly passing clouds like travelling through time. No pupils at all just empty white space. Two of them had long beard and the other seems to be female but still intimidating, which would most likely be the woman, past known as Loretta Alkala who had claimed to be from Peru; nonetheless, later known to be a camouflage hiding her true identity.

As the three made it close to the shoreline where the summit was taking place, they were clearly pegged at fourteen feet tall and somewhere around one thousand three hundred pounds each in weight. They all had scepters and a strange object looking like a weapon mounted on their forearm.

They were just twelve yards away from land just hovering over the water staring at all the people, but they locked eyes with the leaders more than the people present. Several leaders could be seen shivering in panic while others in the crowd fainted in such shock. The Chinese president uttered words to his translators but before the translator could reply, those beings responded also in Chinese saying, "QUIET PUTRID WASTE OF SPACE"!

The Chinese president seemed shocked at this insult but maintained composure although shaken up at the scolding.

The Russian and US presidents had red alert buttons at hands reach which whenever pressed, the might of all militaries combined would begin a terrible assault. At the very moment this was about to occur, the three monsters launched the first attack, their eyes turned brighter than the surface of the sun and launched not fire but a ray of light with a width of about ten to twelve feet, basically burning people alive standing nearby sweeping their heads in a horizontal fashion clearly to maximize fatality. In an instant, hundreds of people were turned to piles of ashes. Not even bones remained and the stench of burning flesh was horrific. At that moment, the earth's military was unleashed in a mega retaliation. People ran everywhere for cover, some clearly injured while others had already been killed. Massive machine gun fire was opened from nearby ships off the coast as well as air power. Several torpedoes launched from submarines from over twenty miles under the sea. The entire area of Zandvoort was now up in fire, smoke and destruction. Clyde Harper and Delylah took cover with the US president and members of the white house in a nearby building, but the president decided to step out from hiding and confront these destructive beings because he felt it was his duty to show his face forth as leader of the free world. Hundreds of missiles, torpedoes and tanks fired at will, but when the president stepped out from hiding, the firing stopped. As they waited for the smoke and dust to clear and obviously, they must stop the retaliation if the president is in clear sight.

To a frightening sight, these beings were all still floating there just a few feet from the water's edge with not even scratch on them.

The US president walked up to about twenty feet from them, looking like a little boy in comparison and yelled at them; "STOP, PLEASE STOP AND RETURN TO WHATEVER PART OF HELL YOU CAME FROM! YOU ARE KILLING INNOCENT PEOPLE! WHAT THE HECK DO YOU WANT WITH US? WE DID NOT KILL YOUR PEOPLE! THAT HAPPENED THOUSANDS OF

YEARS AGO AND IT WAS THE PROPHET MOSES WHO DID IT SO LEAVE US ALONE PLEASE!"

To the ears of anyone, that would be a very emotional moment hearing the president of the United States say please and begging for mercy not from the heavenly father but from murderous witches who have already now proven to be even more powerful than the entire planet combined. This was truly without a doubt the fate of mankind being sealed.

Then came out Delylah to join the president being a descendant from the lineage of Moses.

When Jannice and Jambre saw her coming forth, said in a powerful tone; "AHHH THERE SHE IS! THE OFFSPRING OF WEAKNESS! DAUGHTER OF SIN AND PROTAGONIST OF FLASHOOD AND INJUSTICE! WE WILL KILL YOU TODAY DECENDAT OF MOSES, "YADU" AND THE "GREAT SHADDAI"! YOUR WRETCHED FLESH AND PUTRID BONES WILL PERISH AND DWELL IN THE EARTH WHERE THE MAGGOTS WILL FEAST! NOT EVEN YOUR GOD CAN SAVE YOU TODAY!"

A moment after they made the move to trap Delylah in their grasp, something incredible started to occur. tightening pressure and heat began to descend once more from everywhere. Strange haunting like sounds began emanating from over the water and surrounding hillsides sounding almost like a thousand trombones simultaneously even causing the calm waters of the North Sea to shimmer like boiling water in a pot.

Fighter jets were circling above attempting to fire but found themselves completely disarmed. Missiles and machines guns would not fire; displays on their onboard cockpit saying, "system error, system error". The giant Jannice and Jambre stood still with heads tilted upward as if they knew what was coming just before they eradicated Delylah since it was imminent she was about to be killed but no one could see what was coming. Clearly no power on earth could stop this phenomenon because even the US president was taken out of the danger zone into safety. No doubt exist that these diabolical giants would kill him as well without regards. Keep in mind they care nothing about earthly power, leaders, congress, any treaty among mankind or constitution. They simply eradicate anything and anyone to obtain their objective.

About one mile above the North Sea, the heavens opened with a blinding flash of white light yet again, it looked like a million stars combined at close range which appeared like the light of a massive asteroid crashing into earth's atmosphere. The bright light seemed to cover the entire sea and all of Amsterdam. The light was so bright people had to cover their faces and even so; the heat coming from the object above descending was so strong that even some superficial skin burns were appearing on many people, and out of the bright heavens above appeared he who is called "Shaddai" also known as the angel Metatron. The moment had arrived to meet one of the greatest angels of the heavenly father, his most thrusted warrior. According to some Jewish scriptures and noncanonical ancient Christendom gospels, he is the only angel who does not need to cover his face when in the presence of the creator and is also greater than archangel Michael. He is the hierarchy of noncanonical angles surpassing Michael and Gabriel in power and capability. It is said in his true form he is larger than the planets and is given total authority by the almighty father to instill order throughout the universe and among creation of the seen and unseen. He goes by many names but primarily is known as Metatron and is believed to have once been a man on earth, obedient to God and led a holy dignified life in the time of the Nephilim known as Enoch. It is also stated that he was one of three great individuals along with the prophet Eligah and Melchizedek who the Lord himself took them to heaven without dying like the rest of us.

When Metatron appeared above the North Sea, all eyes observed the magnificent creation of the almighty father and how glorious and powerful he is. Metatron gently descended from the heavens above the waters of the red sea in all radiancy and immense power and authority. He appeared in awesome silver battle gear, a huge thirteen-foot-long sword with fiery brimstone glowing like the sun and what looked like headgear with a brilliant diamond stone located in the center of his forehead. He did not seem to have eyes but rather bright white lights looking like the very stars seen in the heavens at night. This being was truly an extremely glorious and handsome creation resembling human form but filled with light. He did not have wings, but his appearance clearly did not show that it was of this world.

When he descended to about thirty feet hovering above the water effortlessly, all the destruction and fight had stopped. People were in suspense and in complete awe with a jaw dropping scene before their very eyes. Everyone was asking one another; "who is that"? others asked "no, what is it"? the heat had vanished but all the people who were attending the summit of leaders looked like ants compared to this marvelous of a creation. He was at least eighteen feet tall and well over three thousand pounds. Delylah was on the spotlight with a mega smile and eyes lit up with gladness for she knew who it was. She knew it was Metatron who came to rescue humanity from a certain death sentence the evil sorceress from long Ago would have carried out. The light emanating from Metatron was so potent that even veins, tendons and blood vessels could be seen through the flesh on everyone throughout Amsterdam.

´ An elderly man in the crowed said to his wife in a joyful tone with smiles not even plastic surgery could repair, "Lucille, it is the Lord our Savior, he has returned oh he has returned. It is judgement today and I was mean to you yesterday when I gave you the sandwich that fell on the floor and I ate the good one. I am so sorry!"

His wife Lucille responded saying, "oh Lester, I do not believe it is the Lord our Redeemer, this guy looks like he is here for another reason; not for judgement so calm down; however, I am scared, maybe we should go home. He could be an extraterrestrial but whatever he is, I think it has to do with those other three bad ones!"

The US president ordered the military to stand down and cease fire although none of them could do anything anyways because their equipment had suddenly stopped working moments ago and were attempting to resolve the problem but with no success. Metatron floated just above the water in complete stillness then he suddenly extended his mega sword forward out of which another one appeared out of nowhere and placed them both in the form of an X before him and then he spoke in a rhythmic and commanding voice, clearly with heavenly authority:

"OH, PAGANS OF MITZRAYIM WHO HAVE INVOKED THE WRATH OF THE MOST HIGH; YOU HAVE NOW SEALED YOUR FATE AND YOUR "HEKA" WILL NOW CEASE TO HOLD ITS POWER"!

At that moment even the dust on the ground was stirring up as well was ripples on the surface of the sea over hundreds of square miles due to the force behind his voice. It was evident this being Metatron spoke with the authority of the Omnipotent. He noticed the results of his great power on the earth and rose a bit higher to attempt to reduce the effect while he spoke.

The giant Egyptian sorcerers from long ago then levitated toward Metatron as well and the confrontation commenced.

They were floating above the water about thirty feet in the air and around twenty feet apart. Janace and Jambre said in a devilish rough tone:

"We have waited for millennia to finish you "Shaddai". You will fail to defeat the three of us!"

Janace and Jambre attacked Metatron with brute force midair with their own swords from three different angles. They were equally matched; however, it was three against one. One of them tried to drive its huge spear in the mid-section of Metatron through his armor but the spear basically was shredded to a small piece of metal upon contact with Metatron's body, while another came in from behind him in attempt to choke this giant being from the heavenly kingdom. The third launched some type of kinetic energy from its hands straight at the body of Metatron but incredibly that energy was deflected with a minor flick of his massive index finger.

Metatron then basically blasted all three of them with what appeared to be visible radiant energy which he used before against the Guatemalan beast who appears to have been entirely vanquished. Two of these giants fell in the water with a strange black aura around their body similar to dark smoke while they fell into the North Sea. The third was still hanging on to the throat of Metatron but without turning his face and huge body Metatron drove his huge sword backward penetrating and impaling the sorcerer right into its abdomen with black water pouring out of the injury instead of blood.

The leaders of the world were still under cover but witnessing the fight between these otherworldly titans. Delylah told them that Metatron is undefeatable and that he has the authority and power to completely extinguish planets and rebuild them. The US president could not believe what he was seeing and hearing. The Russian and Chinese presidents told the US president there is nothing they all could do should these beings decide to eliminate mankind since it is obvious they could do so instantly.

Metatron then blasted the giants in the water below with what appeared to be a gamma ray burst of radiant energy launched directly out his massive sword. It worked like a fire launcher but far more advanced because it did not operate with any chemical, explosive or igniter. It was just the power of heaven. It even caused the surface of the water to burn as if it was gasoline. These demonic giants seemed to be roasting below; the dispensed beam of energy then retracted directly back into the tip of the sword itself and could be seen absorbing the returning energy. The people below began to cheer on Metatron but less than a minute later the Jannace and Jambre giants rose right out of the water with smoke still emanating from their burnt flesh but clothing attire and Egyptian head gear completely dry as if the water did not touch them, but they were somewhat injured; hence, after all they were living beneath the red see for thousands of years. They then regrouped, but this time on the ground in a large open field next to where the summit was taking place, taunting Metatron to come down on the ground and battle them. Metatron complied but when he slowly descended and his feet made contact, it sank about sixteen inches right through the pavement with a shockwave of what appeared to be galactic cosmic waves [GCW] which is atoms, stripped of electrons, highly damaging to tissue and cells, as well as mass in any form, unless composed of elements outside of known creation. It is like a CME "coronal mass ejection", sending deadly charged particles directly to earth. The temperature rose from eighty-three degrees in Amsterdam and surrounding countries to nearly one hundred.

Delylah explained to everyone that it was due to holy presence contacting sinful grounds. Basically, combining heaven with earth in the same reality and that is the reason that we need to die before having access to the heavenly realm. Our physical bodies would never resist the power of the almighty's presence in a physical form, not even Moses was able to see him with physical eyes; although, he did make that request but when he did; the heavenly father replied to him that "no one can ever see him and live to tell about it" ,stated in the old testament, and according to what Delylah had just told everyone, it did make sense of what was occurring with Metatron.

The Egyptians sorcerers Jannace and Jambre were quite powerful as well since they practiced dark magic and were known to mimic and replicate most of the miracles Moses did, given to him by God himself in order to free the Israelites from Pharoah's grip.

Metatron placed both feet on the ground which had sunken more than a foot into solid ground and then raised both hands into the heavens and motioned from left to right incredibly erecting a crystal or transparent type barrier shielding all the people from further harm but this barrier protection was not a tangible material since it moved like waves of fog in a breeze in early morning. Metatron spoke directly to Delylah and told her that everyone inside the shield would be protected.

It was amazing to see such things being done by this being.

When he stood before all the humans of the earth on the outside of this barrier with his feet partially sunken in the ground, he was enormous in stature measuring at least seventeen feet tall and a body mass the size of a passenger bus, but what stood out the most more than anything about him was his incredibly brightly illuminated eyes.

They were as if looking at two extremely bright stars in the heavens on a dark night at very close range. No eyeballs, no pupils no eyelids but rather, like LED lights but a thousand times brighter.

The Jannace and Jambre were about one hundred yards away chanting words in what sounded like Hebrew with their heads tilted down toward the ground. Before Metatron moved over to battle them once again, he addressed the leaders of the world for the first time after his arrival to earth. He began by saying:

"Oh guiding beacons of hope, remember that ye too must adhere to the kingdom of heaven' for divine judgement is sure to follow should your deeds be ruthless and cruel, as for out of cruelty, evil is born, for he who sits on the throne of the most high has created you all pure in heart.

These fruitless strife and ruinous wars will in the end bring forth annihilation of self, and the evil one will consume your existence from the inside out, bringing forth a cripple world left deserted and until your rotting soul lays in waste. Heed to my words and hasten to righteousness because "the most high" never sleeps and never ignores his creation. Do not fade in hope if he falters to your plea because your desires today may not be what is the best for your wellbeing tomorrow, regardless of how much yearning for such want ye may have

I will today relieve you from the treachery and bondage these conjurers' sons of darkness have cast upon you all.

I AM THE CHANCELLOR OF HEAVEN AND I AM ALWAYS AT THE RIGHT HAND OF THE OMNIPOTENT"!

He then told Delylah and Clyde Harper something incredible. He told them that "she is coming", but they did not even have a clue what that meant.

At that moment the US president asked him where he came from? but Metatron replied, "in time will it be known".

His voice had a thundering echoing rhythm all over the sea and surrounding cities across Amsterdam with visible dust rising from the ground with the force behind his heavenly voice. It was truly an unbelievable thing to behold.

He then levitated a few feet above the ground and moved toward the Egyptian sorcerers with intentions to end them.

Jannace and Jambre slowly moved to face him yet again and surrounded him. Metatron slowly descended to the ground once more, cracking it beneath him. The Egyptian creatures once known as The Volcotrans manifested seven more beings into existence and the floating humanoids from a few months ago responsible for the elimination of Sky Harper had now reappeared causing the present reality to shift into an illusion type environment in attempt to confuse and disorient this gorgeous angel illuminating in complete radiance.

The odds now seemed to be against him and immediately the assault commenced with a large electric caged fence casted upon him, erected out of thin air by the Egyptian warlocks, made of "quarks" or "leptons" which is a negative electric charge with no internal structure incapable of being broken. Nothing from the inside can escape but damage to the heavenly warrior can indeed be inflicted while stuck in this unbreakable fortress. The seven beings floating above ground began firing what appeared to be short heavy arrows called bolts, said to have been dipped into the blood of ancient witch priests cursed by Satan himself, straight at the body of Metatron from about fifteen feet above the ground; however, they were facing one of the most powerful angels from the heavenly kingdom.

These bolts did not even make contact with Metatron because he made these projectiles vanish in midair and then each reappeared' pointing directly at the foreheads of those seven beings, still floating in the air. That was an incredible power display by this awesome being.

It was clearly visible when he simply moved a few fingers wrapped inside his armored glove and those bolts were immediately impaled in the heads of the floating beings brought forth once more by the Egyptians wizards. The bolts went right through each of them with a force so strong that it pushed these beings several hundred yards out of the air smashing their bodies into the ground. It was like a rocket hitting a raven in midair.

Jannace and Jambre then launched dozens of daggered projectiles from beneath their ragged cloaks in rapid succession, followed by a tremendous stream of orange light emanating from their eyes; directly at Metatron, but he immediately blasted his way free of that electric prison obliterating it. He walked slowly toward his enemies completely disregarding that orange glow hitting him; basically, absorbing it with little to no effect.

It appeared that the seven beings who got impaled were severely injured bleeding black water rather than blood just like Jannace and Jambre but still alive.

They were attempting to levitate back into the air but kept falling back to the ground.

The sorcerers then drew their huge swords all three of them with one of them being female since it was the woman from south America earlier known as Loretta Alkala, but entirely different with appearance of a large rotting flesh demonic creature instead of human. Upon drawing swords, they attacked Metatron again, with the blade slowly igniting with fire. All three of them swung with precision skills and lethal blows as well as otherworldly projectiles dipped in unholy blood; nonetheless, Metatron fought back with incredible force with a sword of his own illuminated with massive light brighter than the surface of the sun. while in battle against the Jannace and Jambre, he extended one of his swords toward the seven beings and launched a tremendous blow of a strange white light then turning blue as it split into seven thin rays of lethal beams which appeared to be the very same as a gamma ray beam which is destructive and one of the strongest and deadliest known in the universe. It is held by dying stars and expelled out into the universe at incredible speeds upon the star collapsing within itself. When the light made contact, these seven beings were obliterated and vanquished instantly. Metatron had now killed these beings and blasted them into nonexistence just like the demon beast from the central American jungles.

As he turned to Jannace and Jambre, now three against one; fiery swords fifteen feet long and three giant beings again face to face with this awesome celestial heavenly being; although, outnumbered from the start, clearly, he was far stronger and a little larger.

As the powerful blows of blades collided during the battle, one of the blades, sliced through Metatron's armor and apparently did cut into his upper arm but to the incredible sight of all the people watching from behind the protection barrier, no blood was visible. Instead, a very bright red glow and electricity appeared to escape from within his body, leading everyone to believe he was not of flesh and bones but a supernatural being filled with flames or energy of some kind on the inside sent by the heavenly father to save his children from extermination.

Following that incident Metatron then rose into the air leaving a large hole on the ground below and disappeared into the clouds. Less than a minute later he reappeared standing behind the sorcerers without being seen descending back to earth; however, this time with a pair of enormous golden wings larger than the wings on a midsize airplane. He knelt on one knee, folded his giant wings and upon rising back up and releasing them wide open, thousands of illuminated crystal projectiles were launched from beneath them burying themselves into the bodies of the Egyptian sorcerers and then exploding after a few seconds with expanding energy caused by some type of celestial power. Peaces of burnt flesh and black water poured out like a river from their bodies blown apart. He then glided toward them, some twenty feet away, pointed his giant sword toward them on the ground and the remaining body parts with stench of rotting water flowing, simply erased the evidence of flesh and bones with the power of the glow of his sword.

The Jannace and Jambre also previously known as the Volkotrans were now eliminated and killed.

At that moment, the protective barrier came down and all people who observed what had just taken place were struck in awe and shock with television cameras capturing some of the battle from hundreds of yards away as well as radars and fighter jets which were now able to function properly but had been told by the president and other leaders to stand down and cease fire. Some cellular devices also captured much of the fight, but when Metatron erased the warlocks remains from the face of the earth, he also erased all footage from every single electronic object that may have captured the paranormal.

A few moments later, Metatron opened up his giant wings and ascended slightly above all the people as they were still mesmerized at such a majestic creation by the heavenly father, at which time, several people could be seen walking toward the crowd from beneath the trees in the surrounding vicinity. A couple FBI agents, a few sheriff deputies, Matvey Lukenchoff, Allan Mateman and while to the unbelievable sight of many, a beautiful woman walked behind them. It was Sky Harper, the lost love and wife of Clyde Harper.

Sky was dressed in the same clothing as when she and her law enforcement colleagues were basically vanquished; black business slacks and a light blue wool jacket which appeared quite expensive.

She was alive and walking toward everyone and this was the reason Metatron said' she was coming but no one understood.

Clyde and Delylah were basically leaning shoulder to shoulder behind the crowd while Metatron floating above everyone with those eyes looking like twinkling stars and armor silver gear covering his entire gigantic body. Whenever he flapped his enormous wings, a windstorm would arise stirring up dust and bending trees nearby.

As Sky made her way from between the other survivors and came closer to all the people, Clyde and Delylah laid eyes on her. They could not believe what their eyes were relaying to their brain. Clyde looked as if he had seen a spirit, turning pale almost collapsing. His hands were visibly trembling, and his eyes began to turn watery as a river of tears escaped from them. He completely forgot that Delylah was next to him gently leaning on his shoulder. He began to move toward Sky slowly as in disbelief then increased his haste when he could clearly see she was alive.

The two collided with each other in a crashing reunion, hugging tightly with kisses flying everywhere and tears flowing down their cheeks as they once more reunited after several months of her thought to had been killed.

Clyde caressed her hair and cheeks and touched her as if he was touching a delicate glass vase and said, "I loved you while you were here, I loved you while you were gone and I love you now that you are back, and before this mighty angel of the heavenly father looking down on us all, I will love you even when my heart withers and die."

Metatron gave them both a light smile from thirty feet above holding his massive swords as he gazed momentarily toward the heavens and gently whispered, "Lord; your will has been executed and your mercy to them exalted"!

It was evident that Sky had not been killed as it was expected but basically vanquished or erased from this earthly reality. In other words, they seemed to have been transferred into another dimension but not murdered. When Metatron defeated the Egyptian sorcerers, it all appeared to have been reversed; hence, bringing them back from wherever it was they were.

Delylah slowly moved toward Sky with a smile as a light wind blew through her hair wearing crucifix earrings and Dr. Marten high top boots and extended her arms and embracing Sky telling her that she somehow had a strong feeling that she was not really dead but refused to mention it to sky's husband Clyde in attempt not to give him hope. Sky returned the warm embrace as well thanking Delylah for havening been present to her family when they most needed it.

Weather Delylah had been developing emotions of love toward Clyde is unknown, but they did fight off dangerous robbers together side by side. A few moments later the kids arrived Chess and Lark to see their mom. Lark was still tender years of age but missed her mom dearly. When she saw her mom from a distance across the field, she ran toward her and then stopped, took a few deep breaths, became choked up, lips began quivering, then accelerated toward her mom again and leapt into Skys arms and cried her eyes into rivers of tears yelling out "mom, mom, mom I missed you so much"!

Chess on the other hand was a bit quieter but still very happy to see his mom had returned.

Clyde asked his wife in great desperation and confusion where she had been, but sky could not even answer. She told him that she did not exactly know but that it seemed like somewhere in a parallel universe but where time travels backward instead of forward, that everything ages in reverse. Trees go from tall and old down to a tiny plant. Rivers flow backward, people there are just shadows and not physically tangible and the day goes from dusk to dawn instead of dawn to noon and then evening. Finally, the US president walked forward from an area near the stage where all leaders were gathering and looked up at the mighty heavenly creation floating above with his huge wings completely unfolded, just looking down on humanity in total observation with those bright starred eyes and he asked; "Mr. uhm; I am sorry, we haven't yet met but I am the president of the United States of America and we have been severely attacked by these things and if you had not come to give us a hand, quite possibly we would not still be here. Please tell us who you really are and where it is you come from. I must say I'm having a difficult time accepting and believing everything we are seeing and have been going through"!

Metatron still had not yet said a word but before responding to the US president, he looked over at Delylah and said to her in an echoing and extremely heavy tone of voice rattling the ground and causing the sand and tiny rocks to visibly vibrate, "child of the most high, you are one of the last descendants of Moses, Abraham and Adam.

The Sem priests knew you were alive all this time but your father in the celestial kingdom reigns supreme over all his perfect work"!

Then he turned to the US president and lowered his enormous body just a bit and said:

"I come from the creator! I exist in all timelines, and I can travel across universes and worlds per milliseconds of your world! I am indestructible and I possess the power of a thousand suns and the glory the most high!

I can see the vessels in your blood, and I can see your actions before they even become thoughts! I can speak thousands of languages and my mass in true essence; your world could never sustain.

I knew Abraham and I knew Moses because I too had been on this earth in time past.

As for your aggressors, the Sem priests, were of eons ago, infected with evil of the deceiver used for the benefit of he who was called the name Pharaoh; however, they also knew the might of the heavens and the total power it holds as for they too once lived there but were cast down to the depts of this earth imprisoned by my brother Michael, but in this present day you now behold, they rose and held you as ransom, knowing fairly well that the heavenly lord will never leave you alone to perish at the hands of the darkness!

That is why I am here!

My name is Metatron, but I have many names and I can duplicate any identity I wish, and I have indeed been watching you all from the loftiness of the mansions of Zion; hence, I am at the command of the omnipotent"!

Everyone gathered there had their jaws wide open as if in complete shock and awe while some had a huge smile knowing that there is a creator who finally revealed himself sending one of his warriors to save them from certain extinction had Metatron not showed up.

Before the President wanted to ask another question, Alan Mateman asked:

"Excuse me Mr. Metatron, you think you can help me with a woman? I just, oh gosh how do I ask for this?

Well, I would really like to have a girlfriend please!" he said.

Metatron responded saying, "that is for your father in heaven to decide young lad"!

But then he looked down at Delylah once again and told her, "Oh blessed child of the east; soon your flesh will become two and then one and he will also know the lord"!

Delylah stared at her hero angel sent by the heavens and gave him a smile because she knew that what had just been revealed to her was that she was about to meet her soulmate.

The Russian president asked Metatron in his own language, "why is there so much evil and destruction in the world if indeed it was created by the supreme being?

Metatron responded, "consider how evil has a stronghold on humanity and the battle is mostly spiritual, although it may not seem so but the rebellion occurred at the beginning and we fought and defeated the darkness but as a byproduct of light and darkness, you and your existence are constantly being assaulted by the forces of evil. Even kings and queens, governors and presidents are no exception as for the evil one recognizes no distinction in ranks within the race of the homo sapiens. Know it well children of the omnipotent that ye have always had the power and the remedy for all your afflictions, because your father created you perfect and within thee planted his own essence, why dost thou bring yourselves so low as to fights, dissension, envy, greed, hate and cruelty, when in his hands lays your very next breath?

These fruitless strife and ruinous wars will in time cease to exist and in due time it will become evident that divided you will fail.

Consider how without the earth's moon, the earth will be no more and without the suns heat, nothing will grow, including yourselves and without the rains, you will go hungry for the earth will succumb to drought and without the oceans their cannot exist climate; hence, as you can see all of creation is in perfect synchronization within itself, except for the human race infected with the darkness of evil, alas, you do not have to be imprisoned by these things for you all are created for much majestic reaches the father has ordained for you, even before Adam was brought forth"!

These words fell like a bomb, primarily to the leaders of nations but no one dared to contradict Metatron because they knew they would be biting off much more than they could chew.

Generals and military officials could be seen looking at each other then lowering their heads as if saying to one another, it is all very real and it is the bare truth, but Metatron was not saying these things to lecture humanity, he was passing on a divine ordinance with authority of the almighty lord.

Matvey Lukenchoff asked Metatron why did the atmosphere became overheated as soon as he made his arrival?

Metatron answered, "I bring the warmth of the lord into your world from Zion!

Your world has rules and is bound by time and space. Friction always exists when the laws of your physics are broken or violated but the heavenly kingdom has nothing as such; therefore, we were created to exist everywhere and in any form. This is why your earthly terrestrial reality needs to perish in order to enter our world. Without the passage of death, your bodies would crumble and disintegrate by the power and glorious warmth that exists in Zion."

The US president walked a little closer to Metatron and stared with peculiarity at the massive being up above and asked him yet another thing with curiosity. He asked:

"What can we do to make our lives more peaceful here on earth and what in the world was that other creature that came out of the Guatemalan jungles?"

Metatron responded saying, "if you fight each other, it is the same as telling the almighty he committed an error in his majestic creation. In order to be children of his household, you need to love and accept one another as brothers and sisters even while in discord; hence, while you occupy this land of dust and bones so that you are not shunned away and cast aside from the grace of him in your darkest moments and in your glorious times.

If you earth dwellers surpass the oppression of differences, greed and childish behavior, rest assured that there is nothing in absolute that can suppress your greatest desires from being granted, so long the father in heaven allows your desires without causing greater harm.

As for the creature from the southern region, I say unto you, do not create malicious entities out of tenacity and fortitude for the mind holds the power to bring forth one's own demise as well as success. This creature was born out of centuries of cultural projection from within the entire region; lived within the shadows of the town suburbs acquiring demonic power. When reached its full potential, it was unstoppable by man. Its dark nature was attracted by that of [Heka magic] used by the high priests of the pharaoh; hence, pursuing them wherever they made their presence felt.

As evidently it is now known that every evil and darkened idle thought attracts a dark presence, eventually taking on a life form of its own; a dark spirit or entity if you will, unstoppable by mankind. Your weapons have no effects on these beings because they are not of this world"!

A US general asked; "how was it that you were able to defeat that thing and where did it go? There was nothing left of it. You basically erased him from the face of the earth."

Metatron responded saying, "there is nothing I cannot do. I possess universal authority from the creator, and you do as well but you must dwell in his command and comfort. Armed with the power of his love for you in thy heart, nothing can ever harm you or deter you, even if the entire world rises against you, they will be powerless to defeat you"!

A moment later, no less than two minutes, a huge thunderous sound echoed from all corners of the planet. Metatron said, "that is our father who is in heaven and who is everywhere stating his pleasing with his children of earth being rescued from the grasp of beasts and dark magic. Rest assured, the decimation and upheaval they could have inflicted upon the earth was total; followed by complete annihilation but, that was not their intention.

They invoked [The Prince of Presence]!

[The voice of God]!

[Chancellor of heaven] using all of you as ransom for they knew I would not respond without reasonable motive.

They wanted vengeance for the actions of the great [Moshe] who led the children of the Lord out of Egypt by the power of the almighty"!

Everyone standing there covering the entire stadium, including many world leaders, by the thousands, could not believe what they were witnessing and hearing. It was indeed the most incredible history in humanity now knowing very clearly that mankind has never been on its own and that there is always the eyes of the merciful, keeping a constant watch over all of us here on earth.

Sky and Clyde Harper hugged each other in great love and affection witnessing such majestic display and glorious occurrence, along with their kids and the presidents of the world who turned to each other and nodded their heads as if in shame for prior childish behaviors for the grasp of power and wealth when they were not even in control of their next breath.

Delylah stood alone just behind the crowds but not for too long because Clyde Harpers younger brother by the name of Blake made his way toward the crowd from between buildings dressed in his pilot suit. Blake was a fighter pilot of noble bloodlines originating from Persian dynasty from his mother's side but American born. He approached his brother Clyde and sister-in-law sky saying, "welcome back sis; we all thought you were toast. does anyone have a partner for me here today? I just attempted to save the world but for the first time ever, I could not! Sorry"!

As he glanced up at the [Prince of Presence], he slightly and respectfully bowed in reverence to such a celestial and heavenly being.

Clyde and Sky said, "you know what Blake, there is someone we would like you to meet.

They all walked over to where Delylah stood and introduced them. They both shook hands and when they did, a static charge of electricity emerged from the collision of both hands coming into contact giving them a minor jolt. Blake had a mega smile on his face because he had been single for many years and basically living in military hangers. He had never been in love before, but this is one that was ordained by the farther as it was foretold just hours prior.

Delyah was a very attractive woman with jet black hair and deep piercing eyes with long trench leather coat and a red burette with an Egyptian hieroglyphic.

Delylah was trained in lethal hand to hand combat in the deserts of Egypt by her dad who was a Greek descendant of legends in the spartan chronology centuries ago.

Blake and Delylah seemed to fit in with each other like two pieces of puzzle perfectly fit for each other.

What Metatron said came to fruition in less than a single day.

Delylah looked up at him and gracefully walked toward him almost beneath him as he floated in the air above everyone and bowed in reverence for she knew he was a holy being sent by the Alpha supreme being to assist his creation from certain extermination.

Metatron in response, lowered himself to just a few inches above the ground extended his giant glowing arm covered in armor and without emotion on his radiant and intimidating face nodded saying, "yes you are welcome."

The US president looked up at him and walked closer to where Delylah was and respectfully asked,

"Will we ever see you again"?

Metatron responded to him saying, "I am always near and in the shadows. If you concentrate and pay attention, you will know and so is your lord and creator. He watches over you all even before you were created.

We will never leave mankind alone and we will always defend the empire of heaven.

You too have been told by [the son of man your lord] that in his kingdom "there are many mansions" and his kingdom perishes not!

Out of the dust you were brought forth and to dust you shall return. The jewel of your reality; however, will attain his glorious presence in the realm of "Zion"!

The president listened attentively with great wonder as if visualizing the words being told to him.

Then he asked, "why the high heat during your presence and arrival"?

Metatron responded, "heat is felt here on earth but in Zion, it is admiration, loyalty, devotion, reverence, and unquenchable love for the creator, inflamed with the radiance and power given by him. This power and love transfers into heat in this realm but it is not heat of fire but warmth that exists in the heavens".

News cameras were capturing everything from all angles, hundreds of television stations but much of what was captured was somehow deleted from most equipment by the "Prince of Presence".

The Russian president was passing notes to his generals also present in combined efforts to stabilize the planet which effectively, was never ever seen in history participating as if he was a NATO member, but due to the scope of the occurrence referred to as a global threat, they had to put their differences a side. This shows just how vulnerable mankind is to certain things which though not observed with the naked eyes, may very well exist. Threats never come out of nowhere; they are born and mature into a hazard then into danger.

Everything that had happened was due to what occured thousands of years ago during the time of exodus as told in the bible but never was it suspected that the story did not end with the parting of the red sea and drowning of Pharos' army.

It appeared that Metatron was getting ready to return to where he came from because he tilted his head toward the heavens as if communicating with the almighty father saying I am on my way back.

He told all the people one last thing before leaving, "if you all do not heed his command and carry on this earthly life in heedlessness' with traditional evolution and superficial endeavors, differences and destructive wars, calamity will befall thee eventually; furthermore, deprived from divine blessings and protection"!

After he said these final words, he began to ascend slowly to about sixty feet above and said in an echoing and thundering tone heard quite possibly throughout Amsterdam, "FAREWELL HOMOSAPIENS! LET US DWELL IN THE GLORY OF GOD"!

A tightening air pressure began to be felt across the entire city with a high vibration impacting directly around the chest cavity area. A few seconds after, his body turned into a brilliant gamma ray of light and simply collapsed within itself, then vanished into that light so bright that it lit up the entire city in broad daylight.

He went back into the kingdom of the heavens with everyone on the ground still in disbelief but with a warning and knowledge of a higher power, always with a watchful gaze down on the earth.

The president made the announcement on the stage shortly after that he would address not the nation but the entire world.

Treaties were made not long after between majority of countries on the earth and peace reigned for a long time thereafter.

The End

EPILOGUE

Mankind is still fallible in the end with a dual nature. Physical and spiritual nature which allows us to live in a physical world but originates from a spiritual one, and returning to that spiritual one, while being bombarded by constant desires in the physical nature. Desires are not bad, so long as they do not become a longing because longing then turns into a priority and failure to accomplish such priorities can and may lead to depression and damaged self-esteem.

In between these natures, a brutal battle between the forces of evil and that of the creator are always colliding daily, but when we are aligned on the right path, everything falls into place on its own. When we fall out of place and thread the darkened path, that is when we plead for divine assistance. If prayers go unanswered, it is because something else is being prepared for you.

Considering the planets, they all revolve around the sun in perfect synchrony without falling out of its orbit.

The earth needs the moon because if the moon were to drift further away, the result would be chaos and destruction on the earth. They both rely on each other for stability.

The plants and the sun are at peace with each other for without the sun, they would surely perish.

The animals rely on grasslands and jungles for their habitat, and the marine mammals rely on the oceans, and the earth also relies on rivers, lakes, and creeks for irrigation.

The only species that constantly falls out of synchrony repeatedly with the rest of creation is humanity; nonetheless, the remedy for all its afflictions is always at hand but amid such produced chaos, it will always be a thousand miles away.

ACKNOWLEDGEMENTS:

Special thanks and gratitude to the almighty lord for the talent and wisdom he has bestowed upon me, enabling this masterpiece of a novel to be able to have been written and shared with all of you.

Thanks to my wife Maria for believing in my talent and to our children

Thanks to mom and dad as well.

This story is one for the records and one for heaven!

Special thanks go out to anyone who ends up reading this book as well, for your intrigue and curiosity.

You will not regret it.

THE CHANCELOR OF HEAVEN MAY BE CLOSER THAN YOU THINK.

This world is like looking at a water fountain through an unbreakable glass in a desert. A mirage!

Our reality is knowing how to get behind that glass and discover there is much more than just water.

www.ingramcontent.com/pod-product-compliance
Lightning Source LLC
Chambersburg PA
CBHW040105150726
48005CB00013B/1576